Shards of Glass

Jenny Prater

For M. For T. For all of you.

In real life, you have to let go sometimes.

In dreams I never did.

Long, long ago, the devil made a mirror which distorted all reflections to be ugly and wicked. He took this mirror up to heaven, to mock the angels, but it fell from the sky and shattered into a million-million pieces. The larger pieces were used to make windowpanes and eyeglasses, which was bad, but the smaller fragments flew into men's eyes, which was worse, for they could never see good and pure things through those eyes again. But worst of all were the fragments that landed in men's hearts, for these made them like blocks of ice.

Once there was a good, sweet little boy named Kai, and it happened one day that a shard of this glass flew into his eye, and another into his heart.

Table of Contents

Chapter 1

I lost Kai when we were nine. He went missing when we were seventeen.

He was my best friend and brother and half my heart. It's funny, how those feelings don't go away. He was practically a stranger, by the time he disappeared, but he was still all those other things, too.

(Manda's still half convinced I'm in love with him. But Manda's favorite game is seven minutes in heaven, and I'd rather get a root canal than go on a date, so there tends to be a fundamental breakdown in communication when we talk about that kind of thing.)

Kai never came home Saturday night. His grandma reported him missing Sunday morning. By Monday—

Monday was a snow day. It had been going on and off since Friday night, nonstop since Sunday afternoon. My parents were at work, and I wanted to keep Grandma company, but she was busy, with the police, and the—and I didn't want to be in the way. So I heard it from the news, not from her.

Local teen, missing two days. Last seen snowboarding at 3pm on Saturday. Snowboard washed up on the far side of the river. A

1

glove and a boot found on the hilltop. Local teen missing, presumed dead.

Kai missing, presumed dead.

Manda called me right after it aired. "I know he was—I'm sorry."

"Kai's not an idiot," I said.

"No one said he was."

"They did. They just did, on channel six—you think Kai would go down like that? Into the river? Everyone knows you don't take the hill at that angle, because the Mississippi doesn't always freeze."

"Okay, but Gerda, if it was already dark when he—"

"He's not stupid enough to be out in the dark alone, that close to the river. He's not, he wouldn't, Manda. He wouldn't."

"Okay," she said again, humoring me. "So what do you think happened?"

"I don't know. I just know he's not dead. He—he can't be. Not Kai."

Kai in the dark, squinting at me behind fogged up glasses. Kai laughing as he packed a snowball, Kai biking in the sun the day the training wheels came off, Kai in braces and glowers, Kai calling me names, Kai waiting at the back door with the snow falling at his back. Not Kai. Not Kai.

He wasn't dead. He couldn't be. And that meant I had to find him.

Boots—the heavy black ones that laced in the front. Snow pants—shiny, black, puffy, ugly, warm. The heaviest coat, the thickest mittens, with thin gloves beneath. My ice skating socks.

Two scarves. That hat Grandma knitted for me for Christmas. Six granola bars in my pocket.

Kai was a missing person, presumed dead. He was probably more than six granola bars away.

He wasn't dead. He couldn't be. I grabbed a seventh granola bar.

I had walked across town, down the hill, along the river, and into the woods, deep and deep and deeper, before the cold seeped into my shoes, before I realized what I was doing.

I sat abruptly on the snowy ground. I was going to search for my likely-dead evil neighbor, alone, on a Monday afternoon in January, with nothing but the clothes on my back.

He wasn't dead. He couldn't be. I stood up and pulled out the first granola bar.

≈

I've spent my whole life one wall away from Kai. Our families live in the two units of a townhouse, and our bedrooms share a wall. When we were kids we had a tin can telephone—we used one of Grandma's needles with the biggest eye to pull the thread through the screens in our windows, then attached each end to a can inside our rooms. Whenever one of us wanted to talk, we'd knock on the wall, and the other would know to go pick up their can.

We had to replace the string a few times, and the last one fell apart years ago, but the can still lives on my dresser, with a million other things Mom keeps telling me to throw away.

The last few years, if Kai wanted to talk to me, he'd knock on the wall, and I'd go downstairs and meet him in the backyard. I don't knock anymore—I learned a long time ago that the only way to have a relationship with Kai is on his terms.

Manda says that's unhealthy. I say Manda's a hypocrite—she forgives people who keep hurting her, too. She says it's different because Kai's not my family. But he might as well be. You don't stop loving people just because they become unlovable. I may not have liked Kai much, the last few years. But I'll always do anything for the sake of the person he used to be.

~

I know it started when we were nine, the trouble. That was the year Kai got glasses. It was also the year he got mean. (Unrelated.) He just got meaner and meaner. He had a special talent for mimicry that showed up that year, and he just—

There was a huge rosebush between our front doors, and it made the biggest, brightest, best-smelling red roses I've ever seen, prettier even than the ones you can get from a florist. We were sitting just in front of it, holding very, very still, because there were a bunch of bees around. (Kai always liked bees.) And all of the sudden he shouted.

I asked him if he'd got stung, and he shook his head. "Feels like something flew into my eye."

A minute later a bee landed on his hand, and he caught it—grabbed it by the wings.

"What are you doing?"

He shrugged. "I wanted a closer look," he said. And he held it up really close to his face—I think he needed the glasses by then—but it was struggling, so it was hard to really look at. So he grabbed the stinger and pulled it out—because losing their stingers kills them—and then it wasn't moving anymore, and he could get a better look.

And it was so mean, and I was shouting at him, and then he just—dropped it, and he said, "I don't—I don't know why I did that. I'm sorry. I didn't mean to."

We dug a little hole and buried the bee under the oak tree in the backyard. But that was when it started. The day he killed that bee. It happened slowly. He started mocking people and stomping on ants and being rude to Grandma. But only sometimes. Other times he was nice. Other times he was still my best friend. And I just kept hoping he'd grow back out of it.

(When your best friend grows up to be a jerk, you never suspect it's because of magic.)

∾

I was twelve by the time I admitted to myself that Kai and I weren't friends anymore. I was sleeping over at his house—we were already a few years out from being sleepover friends, really. But my parents have always travelled a lot, and until I turned fifteen and they decided I could stay home alone overnight, I stayed with Grandma and Kai.

Kai still had his bunk bed back then—one bed for him, and one for a friend, and that friend was always me.

I don't even remember what he said. He'd been saying horrible things, and I'd been trying to ignore them, for a long time by then. I didn't hang on to the things he said—I always just tried to forget them as soon as possible. But whatever he said that night, it upset me, more than the things he said usually did. It might have been about my parents—my adoptive parents, not my bio ones. Kai would never go there, even at his worst. Both sets are sore subjects, but there are lines Kai won't cross, and there were more of them when we were twelve.

My parents are my uncle—my bio mom's brother—and his wife, really. My bio parents died in a car crash, and they were the only family left. At least, the only family we know about, because my bio dad was from Taiwan, and no one knew if he had any family left there or how to contact them. My parents adopted me because I was family, and it was the right thing to do. They love me, I think. They've had me since before I turned two. But I know they never wanted kids. So I'm touchy about it. That would have hurt my feelings, more than most things Kai might have said when we were twelve.

Whatever he said, I climbed down from the top bunk and went to Grandma's room; she was sitting up in bed, reading.

"I don't want to sleep in there. Kai's being mean."

Grandma sighed and put down her book. She was hoping he'd grow out of it, too, but no luck, no matter how many groundings and timeouts and whatever he got. "Well, maybe you're getting to be at the age where you shouldn't be sharing a room."

After that I slept on the pullout couch, until Mom and Dad let me just stay home.

I was thoroughly lost and down two granola bars by the time I thought of Grandma. (His grandma, not mine, not really.) To be told Kai was probably dead, and then that I'd gone missing—well, they'd probably find my body before Kai's, even if he really was dead, because I didn't go barreling toward the Mississippi like a first-rate idiot.

We're all she has left. To lose us both in the same weekend—

And my parents. My parents—I'm the only family they have, too, and they'd definitely blame themselves if I wandered into the woods and froze to death when they were both working late again—and I knew I was going to freeze to death. I was beyond numb. I kept starting to fall asleep, and then the panic would wake me. I had no idea how long I'd been out—I didn't have a watch, and it gets dark so early in the winter, it could have been less than an hour, or it could have been three or four. No one would miss me probably until morning—when Mom and Dad got home they'd just assume I was already in bed, so either they'd find my bed empty in the morning, or they'd leave early and someone at school would be the first to realize I was gone.

I was going to freeze to death searching for a stupid jerk who was probably dead already, and there was no way Manda would ever believe I wasn't in love with him after this—or anyone else

7

either, and why should that even matter, when I was about to freeze to death?

~

We live in a cul-de-sac, with a huge circle of grass at the end, where the turn-around is—I guess it belongs to the city. But we used to build snow forts there every winter. Me and Kai—we were the only kids on the block, back then. There are some younger kids now, and I've seen them do the same thing.

It was always a huge fort—we'd work on it for weeks. The plow would pile all the snow from the street there, so we had plenty of material to work with. We'd dig tunnels into the big piles the plow left. We were in there all day on weekends, and over Christmas break, until Grandma or my parents came to dig us out.

Grandma would never come into the fort—she said her knees were too old—but she used to bring us each a thermos of hot chocolate while we were working. We'd go into the biggest cavern we'd dug out so far, and sit on the packed-down snow on the ground, pressed tight together, to drink it. No one makes hot chocolate like Grandma—I've watched her do it, and she just uses the cheap powder like everyone else, but hers tastes better.

I was sitting on the ground in the woods, imagining Kai was pressed into my side, thinking of Grandma's hot chocolate. And I wasn't cold anymore, and I knew I was dying.

Then I woke up.

Chapter 2

I woke up in a little wooden bed, covered by a beautiful, colorful quilt.

I hadn't expected to wake up at all, ever again, so it took me a few minutes to get my bearings.

Nothing about this place was familiar. If someone had found frozen, frostbitten me, I should be waking up either at home or in the hospital—this wasn't home, and last I checked, hospitals were a lot less inviting.

I was just starting to sit up when an old woman came hobbling over from the door. She was old enough to be Grandma's mother, probably, wearing a red dress and a ratty brown shawl. She walked with a wooden cane; it looked hand-carved.

"Hello, sweetheart. Feeling better, are we?"

"I—I think so. Where am I?"

She shook her head. "Oh, you were so cold when I found you. So cold. I wasn't sure you'd ever wake."

"I should—I should call my parents." There was a window on the wall opposite me, with sunlight streaming in. Definitely late enough in the day that someone had noticed I was missing. "Can I use your phone?"

She shook her head again. "No phones here, sweetheart. You're beyond such things now."

"Beyond—beyond what? What does that mean?"

It was a funny feeling. I thought probably I should be panicking, but I couldn't—couldn't reach it. Everything felt far away. I thought maybe I was being kidnapped, and then I thought maybe I was dead—death was beyond phones, wasn't it? But it didn't—didn't matter. I knew it should, but it didn't.

She ignored the question, and I couldn't quite bring myself to care. "Why don't you tell me your troubles, sweetheart? What brought you to the winter woods last night?"

All of the feeling came slamming back into me. I pushed back the quilt and swung my legs over the side of the bed. Kai.

"My best friend is dead."

It wasn't true, and it wasn't fair—Manda had been my best friend since we were thirteen, and Kai was just a handful of memories and barely-cordial sharing of space, and besides, I didn't believe he was really dead. But I was miserable and confused and afraid, and it felt true, in that moment.

(I love Manda. I do. But all my earliest, happiest memories are all tied up in Kai, and I don't know how to untangle them from him.)

"Oh," the woman said. "There you are."

I ignored her. I was—she must have changed my clothes. I was in a soft white nightgown that just barely dragged along the floor.

But my boots were sitting by the door, and I slipped them on and rushed outside without bothering about the rest of it.

I was in a large clearing in the woods, and I'd just stepped out of a wooden cottage with a sod roof, like something out of a picture book.

It didn't—it wasn't possible.

I'd gotten lost because I was in the woods alone, in the dark, in the winter. But it wasn't a strange place to me. I may not know every inch of it, but it was a smallish forest, in a smallish town, and I was quite certain there wasn't supposed to be a fairy tale cottage in it.

I would have known. I would have—this place could not be here.

Beyond phones, she'd said, or maybe beyond calling my parents? Beyond having parents at all?

Maybe I really was dead.

"Nonsense," the old woman said, coming up behind me. I hadn't said anything at all.

She put a hand on my shoulder and pulled me gently back toward the door. "Come, come, let me brush your hair. We'll pull all those nasty, painful thoughts right out of your head."

That strange dazed, far-away feeling was coming over me again, and I let myself be led back inside. It was—I would figure it out in a bit. I certainly couldn't go rescuing Kai in a floor-length nightgown and no jacket. Besides, I might be dead.

The woman sat me down in a little wooden chair, and she pulled the quilt off the bed to drape over my lap, and she sat behind me and began to brush my hair.

It felt nice. Better—warmer, more familiar—than at a salon. I felt like a little girl whose mother was doing her hair, if I'd been the kind of little girl who had the kind of mother who did her hair.

Mom—Mom loves me. She does. She's just never known what to do with a kid. Any kid, never mind an orphaned Asian kid in otherwise snow-white small-town Minnesota. She tries, and she does better now that I'm older. But she's not good at children, and she's not good at feelings.

Mom loves me, I thought, and the brush kept moving, and I stopped thinking about Mom.

"Tell me about your best friend," the woman said.

"Manda. She moved here in seventh grade, and she—"

"No, the dead one."

"Oh. He's—he's not dead, not really. He's missing. But I'm going to find him."

"There we are," she said softly. "There we are. Just you think of him, now, and I'll braid your hair for you."

I thought about Kai, and I ran my fingers along the stitching of the quilt, and the woman hummed quietly, a tune I didn't recognize. And I stopped thinking about Kai.

The next morning I woke up in the little wooden bed, under the colorful quilt, and the woman called out to me from across the room. "Good morning, Gerda! Are you ready to help me with breakfast?"

I didn't remember telling her my name.

It was a weird name. Weird for anyone, in America at the end of the twenty first century, but especially for someone without a drop of Scandinavian blood.

It's short for Gertrude, after some long-dead great aunt. But the nickname came from Grandma, and Grandma is extremely Scandinavian, so I—

Grandma. She would be so worried. I had to go—I was supposed to be looking for—to be looking for—

"Gerda," she said again. "Come along, sweetheart, you can't lie abed all day."

I shoved off the quilt and stood. It was—something was wrong.

My bed was a little trundle that pulled out from a larger bed, which must have been hers. She was standing at a little wood-burning stove. There was a fireplace and a spinning wheel and a few wooden rocking chairs, a wooden table with two chairs, and two windows. That, as far as I could tell, was the entirety of the house. There was no sink, no second room—no bathroom? I'd been there for hours already, for most of yesterday—what had I done for—I couldn't remember. I couldn't remember most of yesterday, nothing really after she'd braided my hair.

And why had I let her brush and braid my hair, when no one in the world knew where I was, when I was supposed to—I was supposed to be looking for—something.

"Gerda, sweetheart, are you all right?" The old woman came to put a hand on my shoulder, and I felt—I felt better.

"Come and help me with breakfast, then," she said, and I did.

We prepared breakfast, and the dough for a loaf of bread, and after we set the dough to rise, she sent me outside to fetch wood for the fire.

My boots were still by the door, and I slipped them on and stepped outside, where it was snowing again, and I—

Kai.

What was I doing, why was I—I needed to find Kai. I was still in the ridiculous nightgown—I would just go inside and find my own things, and then I would be off. I had to—I didn't think I should go back into the cottage, but it was snowing, and I was in a nightgown.

I rushed back into the house. "I need my things. Where have you put my coat?"

"It's just in the closet; I'll fetch it now."

I was quite certain the cottage didn't have a closet, but I—I felt—it was warm, in the cottage; what did I need a coat for?

"Come sit down, sweetheart. Let me brush your hair."

I sat down in the little wooden chair, and she draped the quilt over my lap, and sat down behind me.

"What are you thinking of?" she asked me as she brushed.

"Kai," I told her. Kai was—there was something about Kai. Something important.

She hummed. "You must love him very much."

I did. Kai was—my whole childhood was Kai. And he was—there was something important. I thought about Kai, and I ran my fingers along the stitching of the quilt, and the woman hummed quietly, a tune I didn't recognize. And I stopped thinking about Kai.

She braided my hair, and opened a cupboard I hadn't seen before to give me a dress, and we baked the bread and the day went on. Many days went on, and every one started and ended in the same way, with the quilt and the increasingly familiar tune and deft fingers in my hair. And it was lovely and peaceful and right.

I didn't think of Mom or Dad or Manda again. But I kept thinking of Grandma, though twice a day the brush pulled those thoughts out. Everything there reminded me of Grandma. Of the Christmas season in her half of the townhouse, just the two of us, because Mom and Dad were too busy, and Kai didn't care.

Grandma had a lot of traditions, and a strong connection to her heritage. I didn't have those things. I had my parents, mostly sure that my bio dad was from Taiwan, but they'd only met him a few times. I had six pages in a probably-outdated encyclopedia at the library, and rumors that maybe they would buy a computer soon, and I could learn more from the Internet.

I didn't have a heritage, and Grandma didn't have kids who wanted to learn about hers. So she shared it with me instead. We made lefse and flatbread and kringel, and she told me stories. The baking was for Christmas, but the stories were for always, for me and Kai both when we were little, when he was willing to listen.

Mom and Dad were easy to forget. I do feel bad about that, even though I know it's not my fault. Manda I forgot because the world I found myself in was so different from the one I shared with her. But I couldn't forget Grandma, and that kept reminding me of Kai, too.

In the cottage we made lefse and flatbread and kringel. We baked, and she taught me to spin on the wheel; I already knew how to knit, a little, but she taught me more. And she brushed my hair and sung and told me stories. They were strange stories, strange songs, all with a certain dreamlike quality—I remember them, still, but I don't know how to describe them. They weren't— weren't human stories, I think. Back then I didn't know there was any other kind.

I was happy there. I was. It was the happiest time in my life since I was eight years old. I could have stayed there forever. I could have stayed, and I could have been happy.

There was a closet I hadn't seen before, though by the time I noticed it I wasn't looking for my things anymore. There was an outhouse in the back, and a well, which we didn't use—it was frozen over for most of the time I was there. We collected snow in a pot and warmed it over the fire, when we needed water.

One night, she was brushing my hair—I never did know her name. She was brushing my hair, and singing a strange song, the words somehow both in English and not. I understood them, and I knew that I shouldn't, but they were beautiful, and I didn't care.

I was tracing the stitches of the quilt, as I always did, and my head felt empty in a way that was echoey and pleasant. And suddenly the texture of the fabric beneath my fingers changed. I looked down, and saw there was a patch on the quilt that was black and shiny and synthetic.

The brush paused in my hair. "What are you thinking of?" the woman asked.

"This is from my snow pants."

"It is," she said. "You don't need them now."

And in that moment it felt quite true.

<h1 style="text-align:center">Chapter 3</h1>

I went out to fetch a pail of water for our dinner. The snow had melted, and the grass was beginning to grow, both on the ground and atop our roof. The well had thawed, and we could draw water from it again. I looked up at the roof, and thought of an illustration I had seen in a book long ago, of a goat standing on a sod roof, eating the grass.

It was a silly thought. Where would I have seen a book? There were certainly none in our cottage.

I drew the water and walked back toward the door, but I felt strange, off-balance. No matter how silly it seemed, my brain would not stop reaching for some memory of the story that accompanied that illustration.

A man and a woman had swapped chores for the day, and the man had let the goat up onto the roof because his wife's tasks were harder than expected, and he hadn't time to take the goat to pasture and still prepare dinner. It was a favorite story of mine.

It was nonsense—the stories I'd heard were nothing at all like that. I put the thought out of my head, and I opened the cottage door.

Just before I stepped inside, I thought I heard the lilies calling "Gerda, Gerda," and it did not seem strange to me that lilies should talk, but for some reason I was afraid to answer.

~

Late at night, I stumbled out of my trundle and through the door and into the outhouse, and when I was done I turned automatically to wash my hands at the sink, but there was no sink, and after a moment I stumbled out again, puzzled, for I was not quite certain what a sink was.

When I slept again, I dreamt that I was back in my bedroom at home, looking into the mirror above my dresser. But the reflection wasn't me—it was Kai. I frowned; he smiled.

"You're running late," he said, still smiling, and I noticed that his normally brown eyes were blue.

I reached out to touch the mirror. It tore like tissue paper under my hand, and I woke up in my trundle, awash in daylight. My hair was brushed and braided before I'd had time to think on the dream.

~

In the spring we spent less time cooped up inside with our knitting and mending and baking, and instead we worked on our gardens. There was a patch for vegetables behind the cottage, but all along the walls there were flowers.

It was the flowers that brought me back to myself. The rosebush had just produced its first bloom of the season, and I was looking at the bright red flower, and at a bumblebee buzzing nearby, and suddenly it felt as if I had just woken up, and the last few months were a peculiar dream.

I knelt on the ground between the rose and the lilies—I felt so odd, still, all my memories such a mess I was dizzy with it.

"Are you awake?" a yellow lily asked.

I had thought I was, but then the flowers had started talking—I laughed for a long time, though nothing at all was funny.

"She's awake," said another lily, this one orange and freckled. "They never laugh like that when they're not awake."

"How long have I been here?" I asked, because if the flowers were talking, I might as well talk back.

The yellow lily might have shrugged, or it might have just moved in the breeze—it was hard to say. "We were all in the ground yet, when you came, and we don't measure the seasons the way you do. But you were not here yet when we went in the ground, so it cannot have been too long."

It had been months, at least—I'd left home in January, and a rose wouldn't bloom before May.

"I have to find Kai. I need—it's been ages. If he wasn't dead before—"

"Kai," said the rose. "That's the boy with the frozen heart. At least, that's what she called him."

"What who called him?"

"The queen made of ice. We were in the ground then, of course, but the bees tell tales."

"I have to find him."

"You won't find him here," one of the lilies said, "and if you stay longer you'll never leave. Most don't."

"What—what is this place?"

A hyacinth leant over from its bed to answer me. "It is our mistress' home, and all she has ever wanted is a child to share it with. But children are mortal, and she is not, and so she must steal another, every few lifetimes. She means you no harm—she wants only to love you and be your mother. But she is jealous, and will not let you hold others in your heart."

"No harm—she stole from me! She stole my memories. I need to leave."

"Oh, must you?" asked a buttercup. "We could have ever so much fun."

"I must."

"You haven't any shoes," observed a narcissus.

"It's true," said the orange lily. "Humans do seem to want those, when they have walking to do."

I would have to go back into the house to get my boots. But I remembered—I had planned to leave before, in the winter. But I had gone back into the house for my things, and when I was inside I'd lost myself again.

"You mustn't touch the mistress, or the hairbrush, or the quilt," the rose said.

I wasn't entirely certain I could trust talking flowers, but, well. It was all I had to work with. I walked back into the house, and the woman did not look up—I had been hers for months then, and she was not so vigilant toward rising memories. I looked at the quilt—I didn't touch it. The pattern had changed, I think. I recognized my jeans, as well as my snow pants, and what might have been the shirt I was wearing, the day I left home.

Now, I was wearing an old-fashioned dress, straight from a fairy tale, just like the house. My winter boots weren't sitting by the door anymore, but they wouldn't be suitable for the rest of my journey, anyway, when it was well into spring.

The woman had given me a pair of softer, lighter boots, in bright red leather, and I pulled them on instead. I would need my hat, though, which had been a gift from Grandma.

I went to the closet to search for it, and that the woman noticed.

"What are you doing, Gerda?"

"I'm going home."

My things were not difficult to find, now that I was looking for them. I saw my granola bars on the floor, stuffed them into the hat, and darted around the woman. We had made flatbread the day before, and it was sitting on our little table, wrapped in a dishtowel. I grabbed that, too—the flowers were talking. I probably wasn't in Minnesota anymore, and there was no telling how far I would need to travel.

I ran out of the cottage and away, back into the woods, far and far, until I was out of breath, and more tired than afraid. She had been an old woman, magic or not—surely she could not keep up with me.

Magic. There was magic in the world, and I was in the midst of it.

I couldn't—I couldn't. Now wasn't the time to think of that. I needed to decide what to do next.

I'd told the woman I was going home. But Kai—if I went home, Kai was—

And magic was real. If Kai had come the way I had, then he was caught up in magic, not dead. And he had come this way—the rose had said so.

The rose had said so. Was I going to stake everything on the promises of a talking flower?

Well, why not? This wasn't my forest—going home wasn't an option. Not now. The mushrooms and moss and the shapes of the leaves—this wasn't the forest I'd walked into in January. Magic was real, and I was in the midst of it.

I still wasn't ready to think about that.

I'd come to a smallish clearing, and the ground was all covered in a soft, springy blue moss. I'd never seen moss quite that color before—blue, yes, but a soft, pale blue, not this rich, deep shade— and I got distracted by it, for a minute. My head was all a mess. I'd just spent months—well. Under a spell, I suppose.

There were still five granola bars. My hat. The flatbread. All I had in the world. Plus a blue linen dress with an apron, and a pair of red boots.

Kai could be anywhere in the world, and the world was far larger than I'd thought.

It didn't matter. I would find him. I would find him and bring him home.

Chapter 4

I tried to collect my thoughts, to reorder the rush of memories that had returned to me. I remembered my dream of a blue-eyed Kai in the mirror, and I set it aside, and thought instead of the day he'd gone missing.

I'd gone on Sunday morning to collect Grandma for church—we often went together, whenever my parents worked on Sunday, or worked late on Saturday and slept through church the next morning. They were sleeping that morning.

Grandma wasn't dressed yet when I knocked, which wasn't unusual for her—she was always running late. I went for the stairs, to invite Kai, like I always did, even though he always said no, and Grandma, at the table in her pajamas with a cup of tea, shook her head.

"Kai never came home last night."

"He didn't—do you know where he is?"

She shook her head again, and she looked—she looked like she was about to cry. I'd never seen Grandma cry.

"Did you call the police?"

"I—I didn't want—" She stopped. She didn't need to finish. Kai's dad—a lot of things went wrong with Kai's dad. And he thinks—

or did, that one time I met him, when I was just little—they would have gone a lot better if the cops had been a little less involved. I think he was right around our age when he started really—but Kai—Kai wouldn't.

"Kai wouldn't," I told her. I didn't know him the way I used to, but I knew that. Kai liked being in control—being in control of himself, especially. And his dad, from what I've heard, was mostly the opposite. Kai wouldn't be partying, wouldn't be drinking or doing drugs or sleeping around.

"We'll find him," I told her next. "What was he doing last night?"

"Snowboarding."

"Okay. Okay, so he probably just stayed out too late and crashed at someone else's house and forgot to call you."

She nodded. "Who else is he friends with?"

"I don't—I don't know." Kai didn't have close friends. People liked him—he was smart and handsome and funny and athletic. But Kai didn't much like people. He didn't bring them over here, didn't go out with them after school. If he was snowboarding yesterday, he'd have met up with some guys from school on the hill, but it would be because they all happened to go snowboarding at that time, not because they'd made plans together. Crashing at one of their houses didn't really sound like him either, but it wasn't—that was the only thing that made sense.

"We'll call everyone in class, find out if anyone's seen him. And if we don't—if we don't—then we can call the police."

Grandma dug out Kai's school directory. I went home and got out my own, and we both started calling people, working from opposite ends of the list.

Not everyone answered. It was a Sunday morning—a lot of them were at church already, and a lot of them were probably sleeping. But the ones who were about to leave for church when we called, those ones must have told everyone else when they got there. Because no one knew where Kai was, but by the time Grandma called the police, they already knew he was missing.

~

There were search parties, but I wasn't allowed to go, and neither was Grandma. The temperature had dropped under twenty below the night before—if Kai was outside, he was dead. Hopefully the search parties would find nothing, and the police would find him inside somewhere. No one young enough to still be in school was allowed to go look for the body, and of course they didn't want his grandmother finding that, either.

Dad went with one of the search parties that night. Mom and I went back over to Grandma's, along with people from church and the neighborhood who weren't out searching. Pastor was searching, but his wife wasn't—she was very pregnant, and it was very cold. So she ran things, mostly. People brought food that no one felt like eating, and they prayed and prayed and prayed, and I went upstairs before we reached the inevitable portion of the night where everyone started talking about Kai. About how he was a good, sweet boy who loved Grandma so much, and he was going to be just fine.

They were there for Grandma. Grandma was a beloved member of the community who'd somehow raised two jerks, and already lost one of them. So they would tell her lies they all knew were lies, to make her feel better even though she knew they were lies too, and none of the extra people in her kitchen knew or cared about the real Kai.

He wasn't a good, sweet boy. He was a bully, but only with his mouth, never with his fists. He had taken the last level of math our school offered last year, so this year they ordered a textbook and gave him a free period to teach himself. But his favorite math thing was geometry. His spelling and grammar were perfect when he tried at all, but he wouldn't know a metaphor if it walked up and introduced itself. He could mimic nearly anyone perfectly, and I think if we'd had a drama club or something he could use as an outlet, he wouldn't spend quite so much time mocking people. He was always cold in the summer, and always hot in the winter. Kai was—I didn't like him, most of the time. But I knew him. I cared about him.

So I left the people who were there for Grandma with her downstairs—they would make her okay, or as okay as she could be. I went up to Kai's bedroom. It was a mess, but searched-for-clues-by-the-police messy, not teenage-boy messy. I started cleaning. Books on the shelf, papers on the desk. They'd left his spare glasses on the floor, so I picked them up, folded them, and put them in the drawer of his nightstand, where he always used to keep his backups when we were kids. I made the bed, for something to do, and sorted his dirty laundry, then went down the

28

hall for baskets to put it in, and since there was nothing else to do, I took it all down to the basement and started a load. I just needed to feel busy.

I sat on the ground between the washer and the dryer, and listened to the muffled sounds of voices upstairs, and I said my own quiet prayers, and I fell asleep there while a storm raged outside. Mom came to find me, when everyone else had gone home, and we hugged Grandma and went home too, where Dad was just taking off all his snow gear. He shook his head—they hadn't found anything—but that was a good thing. All they could have found was a body. A missing Kai was much more likely to be alive. And the police would find him. They would.

Maybe he'd met up with his dad.

(He couldn't stand his dad. He'd have never let Grandma worry just to spend time with his dad.)

Maybe his dad had taken him?

(His dad didn't seem to care enough for a kidnapping.)

He was fine. He was fine. They'd been searching all day and night, and they hadn't found a body, so he was fine. We were going to find him, and it was all going to be a misunderstanding, and he was going to be grounded forever. And it was going to be fine.

The next day they'd found the glove and the boot and the snowboard, and I'd gone out to the woods and wandered, apparently, right into a fairy tale.

Chapter 5

I fell asleep in the blue moss, and I woke up there, and I cried myself to sleep again not long after.

I had been loved. I had been wanted.

My parents had never wanted me. Kai hadn't wanted me in years, and with Grandma I was always just filling the hole Kai left.

I was being ridiculous. The woman in the cottage hadn't wanted me—she'd wanted someone, and I'd happened to be there. But she—she told me stories, and braided my hair, and I—

She brushed my hair to pull my memories out; she'd all but admitted it that first day.

That quilt was probably all made of bits and pieces from other kids whose lives she'd stolen.

I had to stop thinking about her. About all of it. At least four months of my life were gone. Kai and I were trapped in some sort of fairy land, and everyone we knew thought us both dead. There was no way to go but forward. Kai—Kai didn't want me. But if I had been trapped by magic, he could easily have been as well, and as the only one with any idea what was going on, it was my duty to save him.

Besides, disappearing into the woods for four months, then coming back empty-handed—I'd be in less trouble, if I brought Kai back with me. Even if I had no idea how to explain where we'd been. And I couldn't just give up, after losing four months of my life to this search.

I noticed after some time that I was sitting, again, next to a rose bush—a wild rose, with a few small pink flowers. I wondered if this one could talk, too, if all the flowers could talk here, but felt unexplainably awkward about trying to start a conversation, if it couldn't. (It wasn't as if anyone else was about to hear me talking to the plants.)

I stared at it intently for several minutes, but if it could talk, it had nothing to say to me. There were a few bees about, though, and one landed on the toe of my red boot.

"Hello," it said in a soft, buzzy voice.

"Um. Hi." Sure, whatever; why shouldn't the bugs talk, too?

"You came from the old woman's cottage."

"I did."

"The flowers like you. They don't speak to the ones they don't like."

"Has she had many victims?"

"Oh, hundreds, I suppose. She keeps them young as long as she can, and her favorites, when they grow too old, she makes into plants for her garden."

"All of those flowers used to be people?"

The bee made a long, buzzy sound that I suppose meant yes.

"I should—I should go back. I should try to rescue them."

"They don't remember. And most of them were children so long ago, they'd be dead by now, as humans."

My lingering fondness for the old woman was fading fast—I felt ill. I couldn't—I couldn't think about it. I just had to keep not thinking about it.

"Have you seen my friend Kai?"

"There was a human boy with the snow bees last winter."

"What are snow bees?"

"You call them flakes. But they are bees, like me, just for a different season."

"Snowflakes are just drops of water. I've seen them melt."

The bee made a huffy sound. "Well, I don't know what strange things might happen in your lands. Here they are bees, with tasks and hives and a queen just like us. And it's the queen that will have your Kai, tucked safely away now that winter is past."

"Thank you," I said, and the bee flew off without another word. I think I offended him, talking about snowflakes.

I would have to find out from someone else where this ice queen, or bee queen, or whatever she was, lived. For now all I knew to do was walk in the opposite direction from where I'd just come; I didn't want to spend any more time in that cottage.

(Oh, but I did, I did.)

(I didn't. Her other children were flowers now.)

(I wasn't her child.)

The clothes she'd given me weren't as practical as the ones she'd taken, even accounting for the change in weather. I missed my pants. But the apron had a large pocket, so I stuffed the granola bars and the flatbread in it. It made the whole thing bulge out, and I knew it would get caught on things and slow me down, but it was the only pocket I had.

Grandma's hat I put on my head, even though it was much too warm out; the pocket was too full already.

Pulling it on, I noticed my hair—the hair she'd brushed and brushed. It was in pigtail braids, and I thought of that morning, the feeling of her fingers in my hair, the sound of her voice as she sang a song with words I couldn't quite remember. I undid both braids, and the yarn they'd been tied with joined the food in my apron pocket.

Well. I was as much myself again as I could be, with the resources I had at hand. I retied the laces of my boots, and set off in the direction the bee had flown.

I walked until the sun set, then stopped. Wherever I went the forest floor was the same, soft and springy with moss or grass or clover, so I could sleep just as easily wherever I happened to be. I'd eaten two granola bars since leaving the blue moss clearing, which brought my total down to three.

Not great, but I'd stretched the first four for at least four months, technically. I would make do. And there was still the flatbread, which really I should be eating first—it probably wouldn't keep nearly as long as the bars, and it wasn't packaged so neatly, which put it at risk of becoming a crumbly mess in my pocket before I had the chance to eat it.

But I'd made the flatbread there. There, where I was— something. Not exactly wanted, not exactly loved. I certainly hadn't been seen for myself, but I hadn't exactly been myself, either, so did it really matter if—

I could have been happy. I could have lived a fairy tale life, and when it was over I could have lived forever as a flower—and would being a flower be such a terrible fate?

All my life I have been so lonely, and in those months I wasn't. Whatever else it might have been, it was never lonely there. And even if I had become a flower, I would have been part of a garden. I would have belonged.

I took the flatbread from my pocket and unwrapped the dishtowel around it. I picked up the piece on top and lifted it to my mouth, and I—I couldn't. I wanted to vomit. I wanted to cry. All my feelings were a tangled mess of fury and regret, and that endless loneliness was seeping back in.

Last Christmas, on the first day of break, I went to Grandma's house; my parents were both at work. There's a lot of baking, over Christmas. Most things we make more than once. But the flatbread is always first, and the next day the lefse, and I help with everything but the lutefisk, which isn't actually baking, and which tastes like death.

Flatbread day was the start of Christmas. We would mix it and roll it and bake it, enormous quantities of it, more than Grandma's stand mixer could handle, more even than could fit in the bowl. We would mix the largest batch of dough we could, and while it cooked, we would mix another, and on and on until night fell and my parents came home, and I would bring a huge stack of it over for them.

Last Christmas, on flatbread day, I wore a red sweater, and within a half hour it was more white than red from the flour. Kai came down when I'd been there an hour, and asked what we were doing, as if it wasn't what we always did, the two of us and before he outgrew us the three of us, on this day every year.

And Grandma asked him, like she always did, "Are you sure you don't want to help us?"

And Kai rolled his eyes and turned to go, like he always did, and the look on Grandma's face was like a shattered mirror, like it always was. Because Kai was her child and I was the surrogate neighbor, because I wasn't hers and I wasn't enough—

I wasn't the crazy witch-lady's, either, and at least Grandma liked me for who I was, even if she'd have rather had Kai. And I was being stupid.

I thought of the end of the day instead, bringing the flatbread home. Mom thinks it's bland and awful, but Dad loves flatbread. He took a piece, and smiled at me, and said it tasted better than usual this year.

Yes. That was a good memory. That was flatbread. I wasn't going to let the witch in the cottage ruin flatbread for me.

~

I walked forward until I ran out of food, which took four more days, despite my best efforts—four miserable, starving days. I like flatbread, but it doesn't get you very far.

It was a long four days. I had as much of a routine as I could— sad little prayers for sad little meals, the Lord's prayer every night because I was too tired to find words of my own, except a quick

"And please protect Kai" at the end. I was bored and frightened at the same time, and hunger and exhaustion made my mind wander.

I drifted into early memories—lying in green grass with Kai, butterflies and bumblebees in the air above us. That time we tried to climb a tree, and Kai developed a sudden fear of heights halfway up and got stuck—Dad had to go up and carry him back down. Stumbling about in massive coats and snow pants. Sitting on the steps of Kai's front porch, eating popsicles.

He was okay. He had to be.

I thought about the day I met his dad, the reason Grandma was afraid to call the cops when Kai didn't come home.

Kai and I were young, and still good friends. I think it must have been in the summer—Grandma used to babysit me in the summer, while my parents worked. And I was there to be babysat, not to play with Kai. Because Kai wasn't supposed to be there at all. He was supposed to be spending the day with his dad, but he was late, hours and hours late.

He came, finally, and Grandma was mad, and he started shouting—something like "He's my son, and I'll pick him up when I feel like it. It's always about being late with you. Maybe if you hadn't called the cops every time I was out late in high school, I wouldn't have a criminal record!"

Only the way he said it included a lot of words my parents were not happy to tell me the meanings of. (I accepted Mom and Dad's reluctant, heavily censored definitions; Kai didn't. That night when Grandma was in bed, he snuck downstairs and stood on a chair to reach the dictionary. He reported his findings to me in the morning.)

Then Grandma said, "You were out all night, all weekend sometimes—I didn't know if you were dead or alive."

There was some more shouting I don't remember so clearly. Then Kai's dad hit Grandma, and he turned around and crouched down on the floor where Kai and I were sitting, watching all this, and he said, like nothing had happened, "Hey, kiddo. Ready to go?"

Kai didn't go out with his dad that day. And Grandma didn't call the cops the night Kai went missing.

~

It was the height of spring in fairy land, and everything was blooming and growing, but most of the plants were unfamiliar, and I didn't dare to eat their berries. When my last bit of flatbread was gone, and I'd walked for as far as I could bear to walk, when my stomach ached and my legs ached and I was too tired and hungry to do anything else, I sat down on a stump.

Maybe I would have to brave the berries, after all. I couldn't run away from home, get kidnapped, discover magic existed, and escape, then roll over and die less than a week later.

There were a lot of things to figure out. But they—they could wait. It was nearly night, and I was so tired.

~

I woke to the feeling of something tugging on my hair, and sat up in a panic—it was the hairbrush, she was going to pull all the memories right out of my head.

"Oh," said a large black crow. "You aren't dead."

"Not as far as I know."

The crow made a sound like a sigh. "Oh, well. Lingonberries for breakfast, then."

"You were going to eat me?"

"Why not? You wouldn't have felt it, if you were dead."

I supposed that was true. And lingonberries—Grandma had lingonberry jam sometimes. That was something I could eat. (I thought they were a fall fruit, like blueberries, but, well. Magic.)

"Would you mind showing me which ones are the lingonberries?" I asked the crow.

(If flowers and bumblebees could talk, a crow seemed only natural. I wasn't sure if I was handling things exceptionally well, or if I'd just spent the last several days in a state of shock. Or if my time with the witch, my little fairy tale life, had simply adjusted my expectations, as hazy and strange as it all seemed from a few miles away.)

(I decided not to think about it.)

The crow showed me the lingonberries—there were bushes and bushes and bushes of them.

"There are strawberries nearby, too," he offered.

"You're being very helpful about keeping me alive, considering you wanted to eat me."

He turned his beak up at me. "It doesn't do to waste meat, but that doesn't mean I want anyone dead."

"I'm sorry. I would love to know where the strawberries are; I haven't been able to find anything I recognized here."

"Well, the strawberries are shy; they tend to hide from strangers."

I stuffed my apron pocket full of lingonberries and strawberries, then went back to sit on my stump, and the crow sat beside me. He talked at great length about his girlfriend, as I ate.

"My love lives in a nest on a branch just outside the palace. She is the most lovely of crows ever to fly, so perfect that even you, a foolish little mortal who hasn't wings or feathers, would be stunned by her beauty." He paused. "I don't mean to insult you, of course. I am sure that in many matters of concern to yourself, you are quite wise. But you are only a human, and have not likely taken steps to resolve your ignorance in matters of ravenly beauty."

"It hasn't been a priority for me," I admitted, and the crow went on.

"Soon we will build a new nest together, and in it she will lay my eggs. They will be the best eggs ever laid, I am sure, for whatever my love strives to do, she does it perfectly, always, and without even need for practice."

He went on for several minutes.

"I don't suppose you've seen my friend Kai?" I asked, when he seemed to be winding down.

"Oh, I might have. I might have. I see a lot of things. Tell me, what is a kai?"

"Kai is a boy my age. He might have come through here, oh, four or five months ago, or really any time since. He's about my height, and his hair is blonde." Kai looks like a prince out of a fairy tale. He's got this wavy golden hair, and a square jaw, and really warm brown eyes, even though he's not a warm person at all. (Or wasn't. We're still learning who he is now—I think those eyes belong to the person he was supposed to be.)

"I have seen him," said the crow, "I have. I'm quite certain. Now, let me think. Let me think."

We sat in silence for several minutes while he thought. I ate more strawberries.

"Oh, I know! That must be the new prince."

"A prince? Kai?"

The crow nodded decisively. "I'm certain of it. Our princess is the most beautiful woman in the world, and the smartest, too. She's read every newspaper written."

"Every one?"

"All of them, in all the languages. She's very smart, our princess. She left the forest when she was young, to go to a place called College, and when she came home she brought many new things with her. She has ruled us well for years beyond counting, but finally she grew lonely, and decided to take a husband."

"You think Kai married an old lady?"

That seemed unlikely—Kai was exceptionally shallow. There wasn't a physical failing he wouldn't mock you for—except glasses, because he wore them. There wasn't any kind of perceived failing he wouldn't mock you for, really; Kai was a master of mockery, and he didn't care for people. It didn't make sense for him to marry anyone at all, but especially an old lady.

Unless he was under a spell, like me, with my old lady.

"She would only have the smartest of men," the crow said. "They held contests for it."

Kai was smart. Well, mostly. He had a very analytical mind; he was smart about facts. He had trouble with things like essay writing, where we had to interpret a text or an event. He liked things to be black and white.

Would a newspaper princess be black and white enough for Kai?

"Can you take me to the princess?" I asked.

"Of course. I was going there anyway to meet my love."

There was, apparently, still more to be said about his girlfriend; he talked for the whole walk there. Well, walk for me. Flight for him. It was just as well; if he hadn't been talking to me he might not have paid enough attention to fly slow enough and low enough for me to follow.

~

I used to make newspaper hats with Kai. We'd fold them following a diagram in a book we'd found, and our hands would go dark with run-off from the ink. We liked to be pirates or captains or explorers in those hats, which meant they never lasted long. We kept taking them out in the rain or the snow, and they'd disintegrate on our heads.

The house reminded me of that. An origami mansion, all made out of old newsprint. (It must never rain there. Or maybe it's magic.)

"This is where the princess lives?"

"The princess, and your Prince Kai, and my love, as well."

"So after she reads every newspaper in the world, she just uses them to build additions onto her house?" Great. Kai had been enchanted by a hoarder and a pedophile—he'd only just turned seventeen.

(He'd just turned seventeen when he went missing, and me after him. He'd been seventeen for months now.)

(That still made any old ladies marrying him pedos.)

"Are you ready to go in?" the crow asked.

"No." It had been hard enough getting out of my own enchantment. I had no idea what to expect here, and Kai wasn't exactly cooperative even when he wasn't under a love spell or something. Better to wait until I could sneak around, try to find him without ever encountering the princess.

"As you please," the crow said. "I have a date to keep." And he flew away.

I was still hungry, and exhausted with it—the berries were good, and I'd eaten so many of them, but it had been days since I'd had any real protein. I walked around the entire newsprint mansion once—it was a palace, really, with turrets and everything. There were lots of doors, or at least what looked like doors; it was dizzying, after a while, staring too intently at something all made up of tiny writing. The edges started blurring together.

One turret was noticeably taller than all the others, and I was quite certain, for some reason, that it was where the princess would sleep. I would go in late at night, then, and try to get Kai out of bed without waking her.

It never did get really, properly dark here. The moon had been huge and full for all the nights I'd spent in the forest so far, and there seemed to be more stars than sky. And newspaper was thin, see-through. The light of the moon and stars would shine through, and I would find my way easily to Kai.

It all seemed very simple in my head, and I was very tired, so I went back to the edges of the forest to rest.

~

I dreamt that day of a little cottage in the woods where all was peaceful and still. I dreamt I woke in the morning, and slid my trundle bed back in its place beneath my mother's, and joined her in making breakfast.

We spent our morning at yarn-work, as we often did, Mother at the spinning-wheel while I knitted from the yarn she'd made. I was making a shawl, for winter would be upon us soon, and Mother's best shawl was old and worn.

We set aside our work to eat at midday, and after went out into the yard, for winter would soon be upon us, and there was work yet to be done, firewood to prepare and foods to pick and preserve, and a hundred little tasks that we must finish before the snow finished them for us.

In the evening Mother brushed and braided my hair as she sang a song from her childhood, in the days when the earth was young and the rules not yet set. We pulled out my little trundle bed, and I went to the outhouse before putting on my nightgown, but as I stepped in, the outhouse transformed.

It had become a cold, white place, with all surfaces shiny and reflective. And standing in front of me was a girl with dark hair and two braids. I reached out to touch her, and she reached back, but I felt only glass beneath my fingers.

I remembered suddenly what a mirror was, and who I was, and the mirror shattered then crumbled like sand beneath my fingers.

I woke up, and the hand that had touched the mirror ached, but there was no time to think of that. The sun had set, and I had Kai to rescue.

Chapter 6

My adventure in the newsprint palace started off as I had planned. The night sky was light enough that I could easily see my way. There was a door quite near the tower I was aiming for, and I encountered no trouble until I reached the base of the tower, which was also the base of a long spiral staircase.

I had seen the palace from the outside. I had known that it was several stories high. Somehow it had not occurred to me that I would have to go to the second and third and fourth stories, and put all my weight on floors that were quite clearly made of nothing but paper.

Oh, well. If it couldn't support my weight, and I brought the whole house down, at least I should be able to smuggle Kai out in the resulting chaos.

I held my breath and set one foot on the lowest step, and then the other. The stair held. I took another step, and another.

Magic. I would have to stop being surprised.

It seemed to take years to climb that spiral stair, though I doubt it was more than a few minutes. And at the very top was a little round room filled mostly by a bed, and in that bed two people were sleeping.

The one nearest me had a head of wavy golden hair, and the curve of a nose I knew, and I reached out to touch his shoulder.

The man who rolled over had skin a few shades darker than Kai's, and a pointed chin, and light blue eyes. He sat up, and as he did, the room was flooded with light, and the princess woke, too.

She was not an old woman—magic again, I suppose, or just a bird not understanding the human lifespan. She looked a few years older than me, though it was hard to judge, for the left side of her face was covered in newsprint. She had a great deal of curly brown hair, and her hands were stained dark with newspaper ink, like mine and Kai's when we had made our hats.

"What are you doing in our bedchamber?" she asked.

"I'm looking for my friend. A crow told me he might be here." I realized as I said it how utterly ridiculous it sounded, but the princess didn't look as if she thought me crazy. (Well, she was living in a newspaper palace.)

"You've lost someone dear to you," the prince said, and I nodded.

"Poor child," said the princess. "Come sit down, and tell us about him. I have read every newspaper in the world, and my husband is very smart. Perhaps we can help you find him."

I was wary of enchantment still, but the princess with her newspaper face looked so unexpectedly kind, and it had been such a very difficult few days. I sat.

"His name is Kai, and he disappeared last winter."

The princess clapped her hands. "Oh, I know this one. Give me a moment." She closed her eyes for several seconds, and the text seemed to move across her face. When she opened them the print was on the right side instead of the left, and she said, "Kai Johnson, age seventeen, was last seen at 3pm on January the 23rd. He was last seen snowboarding on a hill near the Mississippi, and is presumed to have drowned or frozen to death in the river."

"That's Kai."

"That paper makes up the back wall of the third sitting room," the princess said. She frowned, and closed her eyes again, and the text on her face moved once more. "January the twenty fifth, Gerda Whitney, age seventeen, disappeared. Last seen by her parents that morning, assumed to have left home under her own power, as there is no evidence of a struggle and her snow things were missing as well. Gerda lives next door to Kai Johnson, missing since Saturday. Authorities are unsure if these two cases are connected."

"And that's me."

"That's on the dining room floor. I take it the two cases are connected, then—oh, I do so love solving a mystery!"

"The real mystery, my dear, is what happened to the boy after the paper was printed."

"True," she said. "I do my best, but so many terribly interesting things fail to make the news."

I yawned, and she sighed. "A mystery, perhaps, for tomorrow. We will put you in the second bedroom in the east wing, and in the morning we will see what we can learn."

Maybe it was foolish to agree, when I was fresh out of enchantment and kidnapping, but I liked the newspaper princess, and my head wasn't feeling strange and distant like it had when I met the witch.

The bedroom she led me to was all made of newspaper, as everything was, but these papers were in a different language, a different alphabet, even, or maybe two or three of them. The newspaper bed was softer than I expected, and the newspaper blanket thick and warm. I laid my head on the newspaper pillow, and thought fondly of newspaper hats and a friend to fold them with, and I slept.

In the morning the princess took me to the sitting room to see the newspaper article about Kai. It was upside down on the wall, and she flipped over easily to stand on her head, great papery skirts billowing down around her. They were the only colored papers I'd seen there so far, and it looked like they were made up of pages from the comics section.

(Her underwear was newsprint, too.)

(The prince was dressed in perfectly normal, fabric clothing when I saw him at breakfast—I hadn't taken note of what they were wearing in bed the night before.)

"Yes," she said, face turning red, text dancing across it, "yes, this is the one. Come see!"

"I'm not so good with the gymnastics."

She flipped herself upright again. "Nonsense! Here, I'll spot you."

And so I stood on my head, with a fairy princess holding my legs steady, and I read the article.

There was a picture—not a good one. Just the one they took at school in the fall, printed in grainy black and white. He wasn't really smiling, and the camera's flash had caught his glasses strangely.

I thought of Kai the last time I'd seen him—really seen him. I saw him every day, at school or at home or both, but that's not—that's not my Kai.

It was maybe three weeks before he'd gone missing. Not too long after Christmas. It was snowing that night, and Kai was different when it snowed. Better. The person I wanted him to be.

He knocked on our shared wall. He only ever did that when it snowed. I never did it at all anymore; I knew he wouldn't answer. But it was snowing. So he knocked, and I knocked back, and a few minutes later we met at the wooden swing in the backyard.

He was waiting for me. I'd taken the time to get a coat and hat and gloves, and he was underdressed, in the way of all midwestern boys. He was wearing a blue sweater. His hair was flat and damp from the snow, and he smiled when he saw me. He couldn't see me for long—his glasses fogged up as soon as he opened his mouth. We didn't talk much, just sat there together and watched the snow fall.

I'd seen him dozens of times between that night and the day he disappeared. But that was how I saw him in my head, the whole time I was searching. Blue sweater, wet hair, foggy glasses, and a soft, real smile. That was my Kai. That was the Kai I was looking for.

I stayed there too long, staring at the picture and missing him, until the blood all rushed to my head, and I felt dizzy and sick with it. The princess helped set me back on my feet.

"Up we go, then. Time for breakfast, and then we'll make a plan for you. Sometimes even newspapers don't have all the answers."

We ate waffles with newsprint forks off of newsprint plates, and then the prince produced, from somewhere, a perfectly normal toothbrush, hairbrush, and tube of toothpaste.

I probably hadn't brushed my teeth in months. My dentist did not need to know about this little adventure.

The bathroom was as thoroughly newspapered as the rest of the house, but the sink and toilet both seemed able to hold water. The faucets and mirror were the only things not covered in print.

My eyes were starting to hurt—I like reading, but being constantly surrounded by an endless stream of words in any direction I turned—it was just a lot. And my hands were turning black from touching all the ink.

But mostly—this was just so cool. If I wasn't looking for Kai, I could have spent days with the newspaper princess. My eyes would have adjusted. Probably. She was definitely some kind of magic, but the prince seemed human enough, and he was managing it.

When I was as put-together as I was going to get without, like, an actual shower, I went back to the breakfast table. The prince and princess were both there still, drinking coffee and reading the paper. He had one newspaper; she was reading one, and had an enormous stack of others sitting beside her, teetering precariously. She set her current paper on top of the stack when she saw I was back.

"All right, tell us what you know."

There was a cup of coffee in front of my seat, too, still steaming hot even though I'd been gone for at least fifteen minutes. I don't drink coffee, but I liked having the cup there—something to do with my hands, and the warmth seeping into my skin.

It was made of newspaper, of course.

"He was supposed to be snowboarding. He could have fallen into the river, but only if he was being stupid, and Kai isn't stupid. A rose told me he was taken by an ice queen, and a bee told me he was with the queen of the snow bees. A crow told me he'd married you, but he was wrong, obviously."

The princess nodded thoughtfully. "The snow queen, then. The papers don't know about her. I'm afraid I have no real advice, except to keep moving north. You're unlikely to find her before the snow falls, but the weather changes quickly here, and you'll be in winter lands soon enough."

"Who—who is the snow queen?"

The princess frowned. "No one knows, really."

"A fairy story, I suppose," offered the prince, "but we're in fairy land—any stories told here will be fairy stories by default."

"I've certainly never heard tell of her kidnapping human children before. But she isn't the sort one invites to afternoon tea, or even the sort one gossips about with whoever one does invite to afternoon tea. There's no telling what she might do or want or even exactly what she might be; you must be careful, Gerda."

"I will be."

"Good. Now, then. You must stay until tomorrow morning, at least. You need to rest and to bathe, and I must have time to gather the supplies you'll need. Food, and transportation, and warmer clothing for your journey into winter."

"Oh, I don't, I mean, you don't have to—"

"Of course I do," she said firmly, as if providing extensive supplies to a stranger who'd snuck into your bedroom the night before was just what one did. "But first I must read my papers for the day—you may read too, or you may explore, or you may have a bath."

I opted for the bath. Which was, naturally, made of newspaper. There was a little rubber duck—well, a little newspaper duck—which floated around, and a little newspaper soap dish. But the soap was normal enough, and the water, and the endless sea of bubbles. It was the biggest tub I'd ever seen, longer than I was tall, and at least three times deeper than the one at home.

It was an enchanted tub, I think—aside from being made of paper but not falling apart, the water always stayed perfectly clear and clean, even though I was absolutely filthy.

I shampooed my hair three times, and thought of the last time I'd washed it. It was in the cottage, before the snow had all melted—we'd heated water over the fire, and washed each other's hair with a bar of lye that we'd made, and it was—it was nice. All the memories of that time were nice, and I desperately didn't want them to be.

If nothing else, I'd come out of my kidnapping with a lot of new skills. Spinning wool, knitting, soapmaking. That could be useful, if I could learn to separate the tasks from the unwanted memories. For now, it seemed everything I did sparked a memory, and I just—

I wish I hadn't been so happy there.

After the bath I had a choice of clothing—the dress I'd been wearing, which had been cleaned, an outfit made of newspaper, or men's clothing much too large for me, which must have been from the prince. I'd want the third option, which included a sturdy pair of jeans, later, when I reached winter. But for now I would keep my own dress. It fit, and it was pretty, and appropriate for the weather so far. The memories attached—well, it was a nice dress. I could ask the prince and princess for a pair or two of pants to be included in the supplies they were giving me.

I missed my snow pants—that wasn't even good material for a quilt. And Mom was not going to be happy when I came home without my winter coat; it had been expensive.

She probably thought I was dead, now. Coming back at all should give me some leeway there.

By the time I was done with my bath, the princess was done with her reading. A fast reader, but then she'd have to be, if she'd really read every newspaper ever written. Magically fast, even if the crow was right about the years-beyond-counting she'd had to do it in.

(How far could a crow count, anyway?)

She gave me a tour of the newsprint palace. Maybe I shouldn't have lingered. Maybe I should have rushed out, with or without supplies, or at least encouraged her to start gathering the supplies right away instead of playing tour guide. But that seemed rude, when she was being so nice and helpful.

Plus, it was really, really cool. Even bigger than it had looked, absolutely endless, with new hallways unfolding out of nothing as we approached them.

"And this is the Asian wing. Of course, my favorite papers wind up in the common use areas, and the guest rooms, but the fold-away wings are organized by region. You're Asian, aren't you? It can be hard to tell, with humans."

I wasn't sure how that worked, especially since the only thing making her look any different from a human was the text wandering across her skin—at that moment it was across her forehead, and I could see more on her chest. I nodded.

"If there's any family history you've always wondered about, now's the time to ask—I really do have every newspaper written."

"I wouldn't even know where to start. All I have is my dad's name and the country he was probably from."

The princess frowned, and the text scrolled down to her nose and cheeks. "That could make quite a project. And I do love a good project, but you're in a hurry. Oh, I know! You give me what you have, and when you've rescued your Kai, you'll have to stop off here to let us know you've succeeded, and in the meantime I will research, so I can be ready to tell you everything that I've learned."

"I really don't want to make any more work for you. You've already—"

"It's hardly work; newspapers are my passion. Oh, do let me have this little project. Otherwise I'm sure I will be just consumed with worry the whole time you are away—a princess makes new friends so seldomly, and I've hardly even met you before sending you into terrible danger."

"Will it really be so dangerous?"

"Well, I don't rightly know. And I do so hate not knowing things. The unknown is the greatest danger of all, don't you think?"

"I suppose so."

"Then it's settled. You'll give me your father's name, and I will make a present of your family history for when you return victorious."

A horrible thought occurred to me. "I'm, um. I don't mean to be ungrateful, but I have just got away from a witch who kidnapped me and stole my memories. This isn't one of those situations where you use my true name to do something horrible to me, right?"

She laughed, a sound like crinkling paper. "I already have your name, darling. It's in the paper. Gerda Whitney. Your father's name, too; you telling me just saves a few minutes searching for your birth record."

"Oh. Right. Sorry."

She laughed again. "It's no trouble—you should never put too much faith in fairies. Many of us have an unhealthy fascination with humans, but I only care for the words they write. And my prince, of course, though he'll be less human the longer we're married, or I would be doomed to outlive him."

Chapter 7

The next morning I was loaded into a newspaper sleigh. It moved under its own power, and was loaded full of supplies—food and clothing, mostly. The princess gave me instructions for operating it, pointed me north, and handed me a pocket watch in an intricate silver case.

"Now, if you are going north—and you must go north—the only way is through the forest of time. I had not thought, until my prince reminded me last night—it matters little, unless you are mortal. Each hour in the forest of time is worth a day anywhere else. It will take you a few days, and that may come out to months. You must not linger; the forest of time is dangerous, as is all of fairy land. You are travelling, but your Kai has likely stayed in one place, and that puts him at greater risk. The longer you stay tied to one fairy-creature, the more likely you are to lose yourself, or at least your humanity. After a year it is hard, very hard. If you visited me again in a few months' or a few years' time, you would find my prince less like you, and more like me. But he knows this, and has chosen this, and I doubt your Kai has been given a choice. You must reach him before January twenty third. Today is June eighth, and your watch is set for nine o'clock. You will know when you enter the forest of time—you must count every hour that you are there, and convert them to days when you are through, and count every day after. Do you understand?"

"I understand," I said. June eighth—it was worse than I'd thought. I'd been gone nearly six months.

"Good. Be careful, and come back to me when you are done. I would like to know you have succeeded, and you will need guidance back into your own world."

The sleigh flew north before I could think how to answer, and soon the newspaper princess was out of sight, and soon after the newspaper palace disappeared as well.

The forest I had woken up in when I first left home had ended at the edge of the princess' land, and ahead of me were clear fields and rolling hills, with only a few trees scattered here and there. When I had been travelling a little while, a large crow landed on the edge of the sleigh.

"Did you find your friend?" he asked me.

"Not yet, but I think I know where he is."

"And where is that?"

"With the snow queen."

The crow's feathers puffed up, and he nearly fell off the sleigh. "Are you quite sure you want him back?"

"Quite sure."

"Well. I'll say a prayer for your soul the next time I fly past a church." He took to the sky, and was gone before I'd processed his words.

The words were frightening, when I had processed them, but I—how reliable was the crow, really? The prince hadn't looked much like Kai.

But maybe it's not fair to expect crows to tell people apart—I can't tell crows apart. And Kai and the prince did have the same hair color and style—sometimes before I get to know people very well I tell them apart mostly by their hair. Not that I meet new people very often.

I was going to be worrying about the snow queen—and the forest of time—no matter how reliable the crow was. And the landscape was pretty, but static—I needed a distraction.

I started unpacking the bags the princess had sent with me. There was clothing, most of which must have come from the prince, since it was all too big for me. Probably the princess' paper clothing wouldn't travel well. But there were pants and sweaters and many pairs of thick socks.

(There wasn't any underwear. Maybe fairies didn't wear underwear? No, I'd seen hers; it was paper. Not that I wanted hand-me-down undies from a fairy, or anyone really. My clothes were all magically clean when I got out of the bath, underwear included, so there was that, at least.)

The food—there was so much food. Mostly food that I didn't think would keep well, but maybe it was enchanted. Sandwiches and cookies and little jars of milk. Jugs and jugs and jugs of water.

There was one bag all full of newspapers. I suppose that was the princess' effort at including entertainment for the journey. I wasn't sure about old newspapers for recreational reading, especially what seemed to be human newspapers when I was in fairy land. But I did appreciate the thought. Maybe later, when I was more bored.

My favorite thing she'd sent was the cloak. It was blue, a few shades darker than my dress, and made of velvet. At least on the outside—the inside was fully lined with a soft white fur. It hung down past my knees, and had a large hood, and it closed in front with an incredibly complex silver clasp in the shape of a snowflake.

It was useless to me here, in early June, but I was going to the winter lands to face a snow queen, and I was sure I would need it before my journey was done.

I rode for many hours, with nothing interesting to do. I had seen no people since leaving the palace, and the animals I'd encountered since the crow left were either not able to talk or not interested in having a conversation with me.

The princess had said the sleigh would continue going in a straight line, making allowances for any blockages in its path, until I redirected it. The only real direction she'd known to give me was north, and we were moving due north now. There was no need to monitor things until I reached the forest of time, and therefore no need to pull over for the night. As it grew dark I slid down to a more comfortable position in the wide bench seat, and pulled the blue cloak over me, for the nights were cold.

For a long time, I stared up at the sky, which was full of stars like I'd never seen before; I didn't know whether it was because they were fairy stars, or because there was no light pollution at all.

The light pollution at home wasn't nearly so bad as it would be in a big city, but there was some, surely, still.

It was never fully dark, the sky speckled with lights in white and yellow and silver and blue. Cloudy little clumps of starlight gathered like mist in the distance, while stars that seemed nearer formed constellations I recognized from pictures, but had never been able to find in the sky. I found Cassiopeia, and told myself the story until my thoughts began to float away from me. I slept, and the sleigh drove steadily on.

This pattern continued for three or four days. I read the newspapers, and found them less boring than I'd expected— perhaps the princess understood that many did not share her passion for every newspaper ever written, and had taken care to choose the ones that covered exciting events.

One morning I woke to find the crow had reappeared.

"You came back!"

"Well," the crow said, "I talked it over with my love, and we decided I'd best join you, for this leg of the journey, at least. You're such a naive young thing, I do so hate to think of you travelling through fairy land alone. I don't hate it, enough, mind you, to brave the forest of time—a crow's life is short enough without being cheated out of months of it by magic. But I'll keep with you for a little while, at least. There are many strange things I think you will not be prepared for."

"Thank you," I said. It was getting lonely.

"Of course, it would be wisest if you turned back when I do. There is nothing at all of import past the forest of time."

"How can you know, if you've never been through it?"

"I know all things, human girl, and I am never mistaken."

He certainly was sometimes mistaken—he'd been wrong about the newspaper princess marrying Kai. But I was lonely, and didn't want to drive him off, so I decided not to mention it.

"Beyond the forest of time there dwells nothing but chaos and monsters. No intelligent creature lives there, unless it is evil and in league with the snow queen."

"Tell me about the snow queen?" I asked, though I wasn't particularly confident that I could trust his information.

"Gladly." He cleared his throat. "The snow queen is a demoness made of ice, who seeks only to freeze and destroy. She lives in the farthest reaches of the winter lands, but when the seasons change and the rest of the world becomes cool enough for her to tolerate, she will come down to devour whatever she can find. She is like a vampire—indeed, all vampires are her servants. With just one touch, she will extract all the heat from your body, leaving you an icicle, and the warmth that she takes, she spreads amongst her followers, that they may continue to sow chaos throughout the year."

"What do you think she wants with my friend?" (I would process the possibility that vampires might exist later.)

"Your friend? We found him already; he married the princess."

"No, that was someone else."

"Nonsense! The snow queen would have no use for a mortal boy; you must be mistaken."

I decided to let it go—I didn't need to pick a fight with the crow and have him fly off, leaving me alone again. He didn't question why we kept on going forward, if he was right and Kai wasn't with the snow queen. I just let him keep rambling; he had plenty to say, about plenty of things, and a solid quarter of it was probably right.

As I moved farther and farther from the newspaper palace, the sleigh transformed. The paper hardened, and the texture changed. The text began to fade, and its white background darkened to pink, then to red.

"Magic," the crow said. "It does that."

He had travelled with me a few days when I began to see signs of life for the first time since leaving the palace. There was still nothing like a road, but the landscape began to look a little more organized, a little more deliberate. There were trees, and they were all fruit trees, from what I could tell. I didn't recognize all of the fruits; they were brighter, deeper colors than I expected, though the shapes were familiar.

There were a steadily growing number of large rocks, dark and craggy, and all clustered in little groups, spread across my field of vision.

The sky was beginning to darken, and I settled deeper in the sleigh to sleep, as had become my habit, watching the stars until I faded into dreams, with the crow's ceaseless rambling always in the background.

I had not yet fallen asleep when he rose from the bench beside with much ruffling of feathers.

"Here I must leave you," he said abruptly. "It is the end of civilized lands."

"I thought you were coming along until the forest?"

"The rocks are farther south that they should be—I must go tell the princess now."

The rocks—what did that even—the crow was already in the air. "Wait! Wait! What does that mean? What danger am I riding into?"

"Oh, no danger for you, human girl, as long as you don't make a fuss. But they'll have me for dinner."

He flew off without another word, leaving me with no idea what I might be facing, or what rock placement had to do with anything.

I couldn't get him back—he was already out of sight—so there was nothing to do now but sleep. I thought, as I began to drift off, that some of the stones seemed to be moving, but I was nearly asleep then, and dismissed it as dreams coming early.

But I woke earlier than usual, when the sun was just beginning to crest the horizon, and what woke me was the sound of voices.

Voices—I sat up slowly, carefully—the landscape hadn't changed significantly since I'd fallen asleep. There were still clusters of large rocks, but many seemed to have little fires at their centers. It was from these clusters that the voices were coming, but I could see no people.

I looked more closely at the rocks—I hadn't been dreaming last night when I saw them move. In this low light their shapes were more clearly humanoid, and very, very clearly moving.

Trolls. Grandma had plenty of stories about trolls, and one of the stories she told was that they turned to rocks in the daylight.

Most of the stories were...not encouraging. But they didn't seem to have noticed me? I wasn't sure how that was possible, when the sleigh must having been moving through them for hours.

I stayed as still as possible for several minutes, then realized that was silly—if the sleigh was already moving, it hardly mattered what I did inside.

The trolls weren't a threat to me, for whatever reason. So I focused on watching them, on listening. I couldn't understand what they were saying—it was surprising, now that I was thinking about it, that this was the first time in fairy land that I'd encountered anyone speaking a different language.

Well. The woman in the woods had spoken in a different language, sometimes, but that felt different. It was the spell she had me under, I suppose; it felt like I both could and couldn't understand everything she said, somehow all at the same time.

I would have expected creatures made more or less of rock to have deep, booming voices, but their language was soft and rumbly, soothing to listen to, and I fell asleep again to the sound, and woke in broad daylight, still surrounded by little clusters of troll stones. I did my best to sleep more, wanting to see more of the trolls the following night.

~

It rained, for the first time since I'd left the witch in the cottage, as the trolls began to fade out, and rolling hills were replaced by sharp, high ones, all jagged edges and sheer cliff faces. The plants didn't seem to have suffered any for the lack of rain—everything was as beautiful and green as it had been the day I escaped. Magic, I suppose.

The crow never came back.

I was lonely. I took to praying more, long, rambling prayers to fill the time and make me feel less alone. It didn't work as well as I thought it should have.

I wasn't sure the sleigh could handle the hills. It had been designed, I thought at least, for snow, though it flew like a dream through the grass. But it moved on steadily up the ever-steepening hills, and nothing fell out the back, though there were moments that felt impossible. I clung tightly to the bar in front of my seat, hoping that it was the sleigh that had been enchanted to hold things in, me included, and not the bags that had been enchanted not to fall out.

It was a cool rain, and I pulled the cloak over my head, and found it was completely waterproof, though I would never have guessed from the feeling of it. The bags must have been waterproof as well, for though the bench I sat on was covered in raindrops, I was dry, and so were all of my supplies.

It rained in the evenings and through the nights, and was damp and misty through the mornings and into the afternoons, for many days on end. Sometimes in the misty mornings I would catch glimpses of strange, shadowy figures, and sometimes at night I would hear whispery hints of half-familiar songs.

The world was wonderful and strange, and my whole heart was an open wound. I missed Mom and Dad and Grandma and Manda. I missed Kai. I missed the stray cat that came through our backyard sometimes. I missed everyone at school, everyone at church, the random people I saw at the grocery store. I missed the mailman. I missed the woman who took our orders when we went to the pizza place after church on Sundays.

(I missed pizza, but that was a separate issue.)

I was so lonely.

Chapter 8

I woke in the steadily moving sleigh, when the sun was still barely peeking over the horizon, the light weak and pinkish, and a thick layer of fog was heavy on the ground.

There was a forest ahead, just coming into sight. It would be hours, at least, before I reached it. But it had to be the forest of time. The pocket watch was on a silver chain around my neck, tucked under the collar of my dress; I took it out and lifted the cover.

It was a standard clock face. I fiddled a little with the knob on the side, making sure I would be able to wind it and to change the time. On the inside of the lid was a second face—a compass face. The sleigh was doing its job, and I was still heading due north.

I closed it and slipped the watch carefully back under my dress—it felt like something to be careful with, something to hide away. I wasn't sure why.

Night had fallen by the time I reached the edge of the woods, and I called the sleigh to a stop well away from the nearest trees. The newspaper princess had said to be careful of the forest, so I thought it best to start in daylight, when I was well rested and could see my way clearly.

I woke late the next morning, and brushed my teeth and hair and washed my face, as I had every morning, with the supplies the princess had given me.

I had counted the days carefully, as the princess had told me to, marking them with a little stub of pencil in the margins of a newspaper, and the day was July 6th. I'd missed the fireworks.

I paid careful attention to the pocket watch—the time was 10:22am when I sent the sleigh into the beginnings of the forest.

I felt strange and bewildered immediately, and I looked back to see nothing but thick trees behind me, though I knew I had entered moments ago, and the open field I'd left should still be clearly visible. I checked the pocket watch, and it had jumped already to 10:48am.

There was not a tree in the forest that did not tower so high I could not see the top of it, nor a tree that was not at least thrice as wide as my waist. There was no birdsong, no soft, shuffling sounds of creatures moving along the forest floor, not even the sound of leaves rustling in the wind. It was fully, deathly silent, a more complete quiet than I had ever experienced in my life.

I felt like I was drowning.

I checked the pocket watch again—11:31am. It felt like seconds had passed. It felt like I'd been sitting there a thousand years.

The sleigh moved steadily on. There was a dense mass of trees in front of me, which parted like the Red Sea, a perfectly clear path for the sleigh to follow. The trees closed in immediately again behind us.

Suddenly afraid, for a great many reasons, I flipped open the pocket watch to reveal the compass. North. We were still going north.

Of course we were; I was being silly.

It was so dark in the forest; so little light could penetrate the thick canopy of trees. I've never been afraid of the dark. Kai and I used to spend pitch black nights tearing through the back yard, doing our best to play games we'd heard about that were probably meant for much larger groups of people. Flashlight Tag, Capture the Flag, one brief, doomed attempt at Sardines. Later, when I didn't have Kai, I liked to go out to the driveway late at night, when the whole neighborhood was asleep. All the lights were off, all the light pollution gone, and I would sit on the roof of Dad's car and wait until my eyes adjusted, and I could pick out the far-off stars.

(Manda sat out there with me a couple times, when we were younger, and we would watch the stars together, and whisper about nothing—everything feels sacred and secret in the dark. But Manda doesn't really like the dark, and she doesn't really like staying up late and not doing anything fun with that time, either.)

I like taking walks around the neighborhood late at night—Dad hates that. The lighting on our street is awful, and he keeps talking about how dangerous it is. But I know everyone in our neighborhood, everyone in our town practically. And I love taking walks in the dark, when the rest of the world disappears into sleep.

This dark was different. This dark was ominous, pressing in. Usually it makes the world feel infinite and wide open; the darkness in the forest of time made me claustrophobic.

I checked my pocket watch again—12:16pm. Time seemed to be moving faster all the time. I felt like I'd been there for minutes. The clock said I'd been there nearly two hours. Which meant that really I'd been there nearly two days.

How big a forest was it? How long would it take me to cross? Would I come out the other end an old woman, everything I knew and loved dead and gone?

No. No, the newspaper princess would have warned me.

But she wasn't mortal. How much did she understand about the passage of time?

"Sleigh," I said, "can you go any faster?"

It responded to verbal commands, but the commands I'd been told to use were start, stop, and turn around. I didn't know if it understood me, if it knew how to do anything else.

For a moment it seemed it was going faster, but it was hard to tell—everything felt so strange in the forest.

I just kept checking the clock.

1:20. 1:59. 2:33. 3:41pm.

That was the last time I noted before the memories started.

The forest of time, it was called. It wasn't just that time ran strangely there. It was that while your body moved through it too quickly, your mind was pulled back in time.

I am five years old, and it is the first day of kindergarten. Mom got called in to work early for some sort of emergency, but Dad is here, and Grandma is here, and Kai is here. I'm wearing a blue dress with flowers printed on, and my hair is in pigtails with matching blue scrunchies. Kai is wearing new shoes, and he hates them—they make his feet hurt. Grandma says they're his size, and he'll break them in soon; he should have worn them around the house last night like she told him to.

Grandma takes pictures on her Polaroid—Kai and I are both annoyed and impatient. We're excited to get to school, and pictures are boring. She makes us pose again and again until she's happy with our smiles, and takes two of every pose—one for her and one for my parents. She takes a picture of me with my dad. Dad takes a picture of her and Kai. Finally, finally she hugs Kai, and stands on the porch waving while Kai and I climb into the back seat of Dad's car.

He parks down the street from the school, because there's a long line. He gets out of the car with us, and pats Kai on the shoulder, and kisses my cheek. Kai and I walk down the sidewalk and into the school together; I turn back at the door, and Dad is standing by the car still, watching to make sure we get inside safely.

I came back to myself in the sleigh, nauseous and dizzy. I fumbled to open the pocket watch—7:05pm. That half hour flashback had taken over three hours. Over three days. I was just beginning to feel right again, oriented properly in my own body, when my brain was whisked away again.

I'm fourteen, Dad is on a business trip, and Manda is with her family on vacation. School let out for summer last week. Mom works all day, but she'll be home by five, and I'm not a little kid anymore—I don't need babysitting unless it's overnight. (I'm almost old enough to be alone overnight, too, Mom says, and I can't wait for that, because Kai is a jerk.) I'm alone in the house. I'm lonely. I could go next door and see Grandma, but Kai would be there.

Last week, on the day before the last day of school, Kai called me a—called me a—

It doesn't matter. Kai's a jerk. That's not news anymore.

I look out the window—Kai is in the back yard, in a sweater even though it's like eighty degrees. Kai's so weird. He wears sweaters in the summer, and t-shirts without any coat in the winter.

If Kai is outside, Grandma is in the house alone. I can visit her without dealing with him.

I go downstairs and out the front door, and circle past the rosebush to ring Grandma's bell. She opens the door and smiles at me, and says I'm just in time for lunch. Which I know is a lie, because it's almost two, and if she was about to have lunch, Kai would be here, about to have lunch, too. But Grandma knows sometimes I forget to eat when I'm home alone. And she makes really good peanut butter sandwiches.

We talk, and it's nice. I haven't come over in a while, because I've been mad at Kai. But it's worth being around Kai to be around Grandma. He comes in, while I'm talking to Grandma. He doesn't look at either of us, or say anything, just goes up to his room. I ignore him.

I came back into the forest, and leaned over the edge of the sleigh to throw up. I checked the pocket watch—11:36pm. Even longer, this time. It was nearly midnight. I should eat something— I hadn't eaten all day. I should sleep. I wasn't hungry, or tired, but I had to take care of myself; there was no one else around to take care of me, and I had a quest to finish. I reached back—slowly, still lightheaded—for the pack with the food in it. Another wave of nausea hit.

I am ten. Kai has been weird lately. I mentioned it to Mom, and she said it's probably puberty. I mentioned it to Dad, and he said Kai probably likes me. But that's gross. And it doesn't make sense—I think he likes me less than usual.

More importantly, Mom and Dad decided that I'm old enough to walk downtown to the library as long as I'm not alone. Grandma agreed, so Kai and I are going there after lunch.

It's a short walk. We both have backpacks to carry home the books we want, and our library cards in our pockets. I make Kai hold my hand when we cross the streets, because we promised Grandma, even though Kai says it's stupid, and she'll never know we didn't, and rolls his eyes every time.

We split up once we're inside the library, because I want stories, and lately Kai's been more interested in nonfiction. I pick out four books I've been wanting to read, and the children's librarian talks to me for a while—everyone acts like librarians are supposed to be obsessed with quiet, but every time I come she talks and talks and talks to me about whatever I'm looking at. She's nice, but I just want to read my books.

When I find Kai again he's in the grown-up section. The grown-up section always makes me nervous—it feels forbidden. But that's where Kai will be, and he won't come out until I track him down. He's sitting way, way in the back of the library, tucked into the corner between a big shelf and the wall. He's sitting cross legged with a big, big book in his lap.

"Whatcha reading?"

He looks up at me, and scoots over a little on the floor, so I come sit beside him. "It's about snowflakes."

"They have that much to say about snowflakes?" It's a really big book.

"It's mostly pictures. They're really pretty—I wish winter would come again."

"We've got the flowers now—they're pretty."

He shakes his head, and his glasses slip down his nose. He pushes them back up. "I hate flowers. They're ugly."

Well, that's not worth fighting about. I scoot a little closer, and we look at the pictures together. He's right; they are really pretty, zoomed way in like that.

Forest. I pulled out the watch. 3:01am.

I'm sixteen; Manda's convinced me to come to a school dance. Mom and Dad weren't sure at first—they said good Christian girls didn't dance when they were my age. But I said I probably wouldn't even dance, just stand by the wall and eat snacks. Manda says there's usually a couple big bowls of pretzels, and I like pretzels. I don't tell Mom and Dad that she also said the punch might be spiked—I don't even like punch, anyway.

I get to wear a pretty dress, and Mom helped me braid my hair. I'm even wearing a little lipstick, because Manda says you can't just go to a dance without any makeup. I don't get why not, but I do feel fancy and pretty and not quite myself.

Manda stands with me by the food table for a while, but soon she goes to dance with other friends. I can come too, she says. But she knows I get nervous in crowds. And one of the people in the group she's dancing with is Carl, and I know she has a crush on him, so I don't want her to be distracted by worrying about me. I just stand there and watch everyone else.

Carl looks like he's having fun, so that's good for Manda. Kai brought Emily tonight, but I don't think asking her was his idea, and it doesn't seem like either of them is having a good time. Greg is dancing...really badly, and Sheila and Ben are at the other edge of the dance floor having a fight.

I kind of wish I'd just stayed home.

6:22am.

I'm sitting in Mommy's lap, and we're flipping through a scrapbook. There's a pretty lady in a pretty white dress, and she's standing in front of a fancy cake with a man who looks like me. I know they're my Mommy and Daddy, but Mommy is right here, and she's not the lady in the picture. It's a little confusing.

Mommy says that other Mommy is Daddy's sister. But in children's church they said it was bad when moms and dads were brothers and sisters, but it used to be okay? I think that was a really long time ago, though.

"If she's Daddy's sister, why doesn't he want to look at the pictures with us?"

"It makes him sad, sweetie. Because she's not here anymore."

She's in heaven, with my other Daddy. So he'll see her again. But hopefully not for a long time. I don't want to lose any other parents.

9:51am. I threw up again, or retched, at least, but nothing came up. It had been nearly twenty four hours—nearly twenty four days, and I knew I needed to eat. I took out a tin of crackers, and managed one before I was whisked away again.

I am sitting between Bethany and Kai in Sunday School, and everyone in our class has memorized our Bible verses for the week except for Kai.

"It's not my fault," he says. "I can't read anymore."

Miss Ella looks confused, so I explain, "Kai needs glasses. He's seeing the doctor tomorrow."

Grandma said she's never heard of someone's eyes going so bad so fast.

12:33pm. I had been in the forest of time for over a day.

I'm sitting in my bedroom, reading a book. One of my favorites; I've read it a half dozen times.

3:40pm, day two.

I'm in Daddy's arms, held high above his head. I'm flying, like an airplane, and he makes whishing sounds underneath me.

6:12pm, day two.

I'm baking with Grandma and Kai. She's put on her favorite Christmas music, and I know it'll be stuck in my head for days. Kai and I are both standing on stools, so we can see over the counter. I wanted to wear my new green Christmas dress today, but Mommy said no because it would get messy. I am all covered in baking stuff, so she was right, but I still wish I was wearing my dress.

We make Christmas cookies, and put the dough in the fridge. We make lefse, for the third time this year, because everyone at church loves it. We take the cookies out of the fridge to roll and cut, and Kai and I argue over which cookie cutters to use, and Grandma keeps telling us to stop eating the dough, but we don't listen.

We put the cookies in the oven, and make more lefse while they bake. It takes forever and ever for them to bake and cool off, and then we can finally, finally frost them. The frosting is my favorite part. Except for the eating, maybe.

9:13pm, day two.

Kai and I are sitting at a table in the cafeteria. I had to ask him for help with math homework—he's the best at it, when you can get him to actually focus on helping you, instead of just being a jerk about how you don't understand it. And I'm having a lot of trouble with math.

We both have a study period now, and it's better here, with a task to focus on—I try to avoid seeing him outside of school when I can, but it's hard, since we live next door to each other.

I've traded essay help for actual, useful math help. Kai always struggles with essays. So we're getting along as well as we ever do, anymore; it works as long as we don't try to talk about anything but the work in front of us.

12:49am.

It's snowing hard outside, bitterly, bitingly cold. But I'm warm inside, in front of a bright, crackling fire. Mother and I are sitting in our rocking chairs, with quilts draped over our laps. We're knitting in the light of the fire, and Mother is telling me a strange story which she says is older than time itself.

4:06am.

I'm in the bathroom with Manda before first period. "I can't believe he said that," she says.

"He's said worse, and you know it."

"Never become complacent with people being awful, Gerda."

"Uh huh."

"Are you sure you're not in love with him?"

"Extremely. I don't think I'm even wired that way."

She shrugs. "You just put up with a lot from him."

"It's—he wasn't always like this. He isn't always like this. When it snowed on Wednesday—"

"Gerda, you didn't!"

"Didn't what?"

"Are you seriously still going along with it when he suddenly wants to hang out with you every time it snows?"

"It's nice."

"It's letting him get away with being a jerk! You put up with his crap all through the rest of the year, and then he gets nostalgic or something on winter nights, and you let him just pretend you guys are still friends? He treats you like crap, and every time you come when he calls, you're telling him that it's okay."

"Why should I stop doing something that makes me happy just because it makes him happy too?"

"Because it—"

The warning bell rings, and we drop the conversation; I don't have the chance to talk to Manda again before going home.

That night it snows again, and Kai knocks on our shared wall.

I think about what Manda said, and I don't put on my coat and gloves. I go downstairs and I open the door, and I say, "Not tonight, Kai."

"What?"

"You were really mean today. You're mean every day. And I'm over it. I don't want to be your friend at night if you don't want to be mine during the day."

"Gerda," he says.

"No, Kai." And I close the door. And the next day he goes snowboarding, and he never comes home.

He never comes home.

I came back to myself gasping, in bright sunlight, and scrambled to find the pocket watch. 9:21am. I glanced back; I was barely out of the forest, and the sleigh was moving steadily on.

"Stop," I told it. I was nauseous and lightheaded, and the motion would only make me feel worse.

The first thing to do was calculate the time. From 10:22am to 9:21am two days later. Forty-seven hours. That was forty-seven days.

A month and a half. I'd lost over a month and a half. The date was August 22nd.

I needed to eat. I needed to sleep. I needed to keep moving.

The nausea had mostly passed by then. Good. We could go again. I gave the sleigh the command, then made myself eat something—I found a little tin full of soup, magically still hot, and a spoon.

I didn't want to sleep. I didn't want to think about most of the memories I'd been pulled back into; I certainly didn't want to dream about them. But I was too tired to stay awake.

Chapter 9

I woke in a panic, but the sun was high in the sky, and I was safely out of the forest. I wasn't sure how long I'd slept, but it must still be the same day, at least.

The landscape around me had changed, and the sleigh was moving down an existing road for the first time since I'd left the newspaper princess.

It wasn't much, a dirt road just wide enough for the sleigh, but it meant I would likely meet people soon. The thought frightened me. The newspaper princess and her prince had been very kind—well, so had the witch in the cottage, when she wasn't stripping away my identity, systematically destroying everything that made me who I was. But the prince had been mortal, or at least early on in the process of ceasing to be mortal, and the newspaper princess had warned me to be careful of other fairies.

(Perhaps I should stop thinking of the woman in the cottage as a witch; witches and fairies were probably quite different things.)

(Perhaps it didn't matter what I called her—I hardly owed my kidnapper correct terminology.)

I ate again. I'd had no dreams that I could remember, but now that I was awake, I couldn't escape the memories.

The last one. The last one before I'd come out of the forest. I'd been trying not to think of that, not to remember it.

If I'd gone to sit in the snow with him, would things have been different?

Sometimes we just sit in silence, but sometimes we talk. Did he have something to talk about? Was the disappearance something he'd planned; would he have made a different choice if I'd been with him that night? Had I driven him away? Had I gotten him killed?

Was this whole disastrous mess all my fault?

I was suddenly, irrationally angry with Manda—it was her idea for me to abandon Kai.

I didn't want to dwell on that, but there was nothing else to dwell on. I was so sick of this journey, of the loneliness, of the aching boredom alternating with periods of blinding terror.

I settled back in the sleigh to watch the unchanging landscape. When I fell asleep it was exactly the same as when I'd woken up that morning, and when I woke up again the next morning, I thought maybe the road was a little wider, but it was hard to be sure.

Several days passed, the road slowly widening, the empty land transitioning slowly into what I think was farmland—I recognized a few cornfields, at least. Cornfields were pretty unmistakable.

I had forgotten, while we followed the road, that the sleigh had been set to go due north. North, at some point, took us off the road, and I woke one morning in the middle of a cornfield.

It was a terrifying moment—there's just something about cornfields. I'm a midwestern girl; my stories growing up weren't all trolls and fairies and little cottages with sod roofs. Those are stories from somewhere else—my own, local stories were lakes and cornfields.

Monsters live in the corn. Serial killers and wildcats and big lizard things. Aliens, maybe. You walk into the corn, and you never walk back out.

To fall asleep under open sky, and wake surrounded by corn stalks towering over my head—it seems silly, but that was one of the scariest moments so far.

It seemed to be a very, very large cornfield—we were in it for several hours. It was nearly dusk again by the time the sleigh met back up with the road, and I didn't fall asleep that night, head full of nightmares about cornfields.

Fairies didn't approach agriculture quite the way humans did, I guess, because I hadn't seen anything like farmhouses, all this time; whoever tended the fields must have been coming from somewhere far, far off to do their work. And I had no idea when they might be doing that, because I had yet to see any signs of life.

It had been many long, long days of farmland before little dwellings began popping up, one or two a day at first, the number slowly increasing.

The first looked exactly like every little hundred-year-old farmhouse on the edges of my own small town. The second was made of large white stones, with a thatched roof. The third was tall and narrow with square edges, all a brilliant purple. The fourth looked like it was made out of a very, very large copper tea kettle. The fifth one looked like a cat tree, all covered in light brown carpet, with one little hidey hole at the top where someone must have lived—I have no idea how they got up there every day. Maybe they had wings. It seemed like some fairies, at least, ought to have wings.

I had been seeing houses for a few days before I started seeing people. Most of them looked just like people at home, but I didn't see them very closely—the newspaper princess looked normal until one was close enough to take note of the words moving across her face.

They stopped and stared at me, but none of them said anything. I didn't try to start a conversation; I was a bit wary of fairies, in general.

When the houses were close enough together that I was seeing a dozen each day, the road, which was now wide enough that another sleigh of equal size could pass by me with plenty of space between, began to be paved.

The paving stones were all irregular shapes, in a whole wide rainbow of colors, a beautiful mosaic road, and I wished, not for the first time, that I'd thought to bring my camera along when I ran off in the middle of the night after Kai.

I was approaching a real city, then, with more people, people I wouldn't be able to just avoid.

When I was at the limits of the city, I had the sleigh pull off the main road a little, and slept behind some trees—I wanted to go into town in the daylight.

The ground was white the next morning—not proper snow, not yet, but a thin layer of frost that meant winter was not too far off. I had spent many weeks in the forest of time, but still, it seemed early. Maybe it was only because I'd come so much farther north. It was mid-September.

There were people on the road for the first time since I'd set out, when I woke that morning and left my little copse of trees. One of them had bright purple skin, one had a fox's tail and ears, and one had large wings like a moth's. The fourth looked exactly like an average person, wearing overalls and with her hair in pigtails. I waited to get on the road until they'd walked ahead of me, but they all noticed me quickly. They turned to stare, then began whispering to each other—they didn't say anything to me, so I didn't say anything to them, either. My anxiety, already heightened, rose further.

There was a wall around the city, but the gate hung open, and no one said anything or tried to stop me riding through.

I didn't stand out too much, or didn't think I did. There were all kinds of people in the city, some that looked, I thought, enough like me. I didn't see anyone else Asian, but I didn't think that would make me an oddity. There were a lot of other people who just looked like normal humans, even if they probably weren't, and I wasn't the only one of them who wasn't white; there were various shades of normal, human brown about, too.

There was the purple man, and a woman who was a pretty shade of pale green, and another woman who was whiter than white, translucent, so all her veins showed through her skin. There were people with goat's legs, and a few different kinds of wings, and one man with antlers. There was a whole family walking together that all seemed to have tree bark for skin, and leaves for hair.

There were other people on the road in vehicles rather like mine, in carriages and wagons that drove themselves and ones that were pulled by horses or deer or in one case two large cats, I think jaguars. There were people in shiny new cars and in cars that looked like maybe they'd been purchased from Henry Ford himself, and everything in between. There were people walking and people on horseback, and one tall, narrow, dark skinned, blue haired man riding a moose.

There were little shops and little houses packed close together, none of them matching each other—they were all different styles, from different time periods and parts of the world, and some of them didn't look like houses to me at all. One was an upside-down terra cotta flower pot with a door and windows carved in, which was actually very charming. One seemed to be made of a very large pet crate, with vines growing on it, though not enough to provide any sort of privacy to the people inside it. One was a rather ugly lampshade. One was a dollhouse, just an average, dollhouse-sized dollhouse, sitting between two human-sized houses. I watched that one as closely as I could as the sleigh went by— people grew and shrunk as they reached the front door. (I didn't think a house that required a size change to get into was particularly practical, but, well. Fairies.)

My favorite was a gigantic typewriter with the keyboard all hollowed out to make room for the occupants. But most of them just looked like houses, only houses that didn't belong on the same street together. A log cabin next to something that looked like the Taj Mahal next to a big tent made of leather hides, next to a round golden thing, next to a little clay hut, next to three little red brick storefronts.

No one spoke to me. I told myself that fairies just probably weren't very friendly, and I shouldn't draw attention to myself by trying to talk to anyone.

Probably fairies just weren't friendly.

There were large groups of them talking happily in every direction I turned.

Probably they just weren't friendly with strangers. That made sense. Strangers made me nervous, too.

I'd gone a few blocks when they began to talk about me—or at least, when the talk about me became loud enough I could hear it. A group of them came rather suddenly to walk alongside the sleigh, two older women and a quite large man. One woman walked along one side of the sleigh, the other woman and the man on the other.

"There's a human child in fairy land," one woman said to the other, over my head, as if she mightn't have noticed, standing as she was about two feet from me.

"I'm not a child."

"How old are you?" asked the second woman.

"Seventeen," I said—I could see no reason not to.

"Then by the laws of your own land you are. And human children are a valuable commodity."

"I'm not a commodity." I leant down to whisper, "Sleigh, please, please, if you can, go faster."

"It's the market, child, not the stock, that makes choices like that."

The very large man reached forward, then, as if he would grab me and lift me away, and at the same time a young voice called out, "Here! Down the alley!"

I took a chance, and directed the sleigh quickly off the main street. The three fairies started to follow me, but a great herd of what may or may not have been cattle came between us. The alley was quite long and winding, and I followed it in a panic, sure there were market-minded fairies behind me.

After a few turns in the alley, a girl a few years younger than me vaulted herself into the sleigh. "They always get lost in this alley—it's enchanted a bit, I think. Just keep going." Hers was the voice that had called me to the alley in first place, away from the fairies who'd wanted to buy or sell me, and I was inclined to trust her.

We reached, eventually, the end of the alley, a red brick wall with several people lounging about. One waved, and another reached forward to muss up the girl's hair.

She laughed, then turned to face me. "Don't worry; it's okay now. I'm Cecelia. What's your name?"

"Gerda."

One of the adults slapped her, and she winced back.

"Don't be giving your name out, you little fool."

"Oh, what does it matter?" said another. "It's just a little human."

"CeCe is a human too, whether or not you like to remember it, and her name is just as valuable as this...Gerda's."

It was at that moment that I realized I may have made a terrible mistake. Cecelia swung an arm around my shoulders. "Ignore them—they're always like this. It doesn't matter. You'll be coming home with us, to be my best friend forever and ever."

"I—I can't do that. I'm on my way somewhere."

"Oh," said one of the adults, "it's cute that you think you have a choice. Our little changeling wants a human companion, and a human companion she shall have. We have the bunk bed all set up."

"Come on, then, Cecelia, grab your present and get home; we'll stash the rest of this away and join you for dinner."

I grabbed the cloak, which I had been using as a blanket—anything else that was not on my body was lost. At least I was wearing the compass clock still, and I'd slipped the nearest backpack on when I first started to be uneasy about the city. There was nothing much important in it, except for Grandma's hat, just some food and some of the more interesting newspapers.

Cecelia grabbed my hand and dragged me away; I was still trying to process what was happening. It was a few blocks before

I collected myself enough to try to pull away. I was taller than her, bigger, stronger.

She clung tightly to my hand. "Don't be dumb—I only want a friend. You go out there, and you'll run right into someone who wants something much worse. They'll all want something worse."

She made, unfortunately, a good point.

"Besides, I've your name, or the first part at least. I'll bind you to me, and then you shall never, ever go away."

I tried again to pull away from her, and succeeded that time, but I'd only run a few yards when I caught sight of the same very large man who'd tried to grab me before.

Cecelia caught up, and took my hand again, and I let her. She didn't have my true name, not the full thing, so I wasn't sure she really could bind me. And going back out onto the busy fairy street with none of my supplies was—I needed time to think, was all. I could get away. Just...in a bit.

The house Cecelia took me to was away from the main part of the city, still within the walls, but some distance from the main road I'd been driving down. It was a normal looking house, at first glance, but up close, I saw it was a cobbled together mess of several other houses, little mismatched sections jammed together, different styles and colors. The whole thing was very large.

She was still holding my hand tightly, and she dragged me inside, up a flight of stairs and down a few hallways, before she stopped in front of a closed door.

"Okay. This is my room."

The room was—it was a nightmare. It looked like she'd crammed an entire zoo into a twelve-by-twelve room, and also like she'd never once cleaned up after anything living there. The smell was sickening. There were multiple cages with rodents in them, an aquarium, three separate ant farms, and a litter box—I didn't see any actual cats at that time, but three of them emerged from under the bed and inside the closet over the next couple hours. All the rodents turned out to be guinea pigs, when I got a proper look.

There was a bunk bed, which reminded me of Kai, but anything would have reminded me of Kai, at that point. Winter was falling, or perhaps I was falling into winter—I was getting closer, and my sense of urgency was rising every hour.

There was a bookshelf reaching nearly to the ceiling, with a few books on it, but mostly crammed full of just all sorts of random junk.

The worst thing, though. The worst thing was that the closet was actually a walk-in closet nearly as large as the bedroom, and inside it, along with all her clothes, there was an actual, live reindeer.

Now, I don't know much about, like, pet care, in general, but I am very certain that a closet is not the appropriate environment for a reindeer.

"You'll stay in the bottom bunk," she told me, "and I'll try to clear some drawer space for you, and we shall be sisters and the dearest of friends. You shan't leave the room except to go to the bathroom, but every Tuesday you may come with me to play outside for an hour."

And so began my second time as a prisoner of fairies.

Chapter 10

It took me only a few days to realize escape wasn't a viable option, at least not immediately—it would take planning. The window in Cecelia's room didn't open, the bathroom I was allowed to go to was only a few feet down the hall, and the whole house was riddled with fairies. I never even made it to the front door, or any outside door; I couldn't find them. The hallways moved—I'm certain of it—and if any fairy caught me anywhere but Cecelia's room, the bathroom, or the small space between, they were...not pleased. They didn't lay hands on me; it was clear they considered me another of Cecelia's pets, and I was therefore hers to...train, or something. She was scolded badly if I was out of place. But they—when someone you know has that much more power than you is clearly angry, it's sort of terrifying, even if they're not angry with you.

They always made a point of using my name, when they found me. I knew they didn't have the full thing, and therefore didn't have full power, but I was made to understand that with even a piece of my name, they could...not just do things to me, but make me do things. And that was—

So I didn't get into fights with fairies. I avoided them when I could, ran back to Cecelia's room when they told me to, and gave up on searching for an exit when it became clear that the house would change itself as needed to prevent me finding one.

(They never used my name to hurt me, or control me, only to threaten me. In hindsight, I'm not certain they could do anything with only a partial name. But I was too frightened, then, to take the risk.)

The only time I accessed an outside door was when Cecelia led me into the backyard. The hallways didn't move for her; they stayed where she wanted them.

Cecelia didn't seem to have a clear understanding of the meaning of the word Tuesday. She took me outside about a week after I'd gotten there, and the next time two days later, then eight days, then five. She also wasn't fully clear on what an hour was— once we were out for less than ten minutes, and another time for at least six hours. At least, we went out when the sun was in the center of the sky, and came back in as it was setting. I had to guess on the times, since she was with me whenever we were outside. The pocket watch on its chain was tucked safely beneath my dress, and though a bump showed through, Cecelia hadn't noticed, and neither had any of the fairies in the house. Maybe there was an enchantment on it; it had been a gift from a fairy.

The contents of Cecelia's backyard included: a rusty chain link fence. A rusted-out car from the nineteen forties. A swing set that was definitely not up to code. An old wooden swing that was rotting all to pieces. Grass that was somehow both brown and dead and extremely overgrown. An abundance of dandelions, I think—they looked like dandelions, except that they were red instead of yellow. A half dozen deflated balls, one soccer, one basketball, one football, and three of the cheap latex kind you find at the grocery store. An alarmingly large patch of thistles. A dead squirrel.

Cecelia usually sat on a swing and chattered happily while she swung. I stood, since I didn't trust the swing set not to collapse under any additional weight, and I didn't trust it not to give me diseases just from touching it, and I just didn't want to be that close to Cecelia. I ignored her chatter as well as I could, and studied the small rotting corpse on the ground that had once been a squirrel. It wouldn't have been hard to just dispose of the little body, but it was there, in worse shape, every time I went outside.

I hated that place. I hated those people.

Cecelia seemed utterly unaware that we were not, in fact, best friends. I kind of wanted to let her know, very loudly and very firmly, but I didn't want to antagonize her, since her inexplicable fondness for me seemed to be the only thing protecting me from a worse—or at least more currently more mysterious—fate at the hands of the fairies that were her family.

I studied her, when I got bored of the squirrel. I couldn't decide how old I thought she was. Fourteen? No, maybe twelve? Ten? It was hard to say. Younger than me; I was sure of that much at least.

I made myself busy cleaning. It felt like giving up, volunteering my services as maid to my kidnapper, but I had to live in her bedroom too, and the stench was truly unbearable. Fortunately, a whole package of unused trash bags were among the many things Cecelia had hoarded, so I threw out the bedding in all the guinea pig cages, and when I couldn't find anything else to replace it, I dug out my backpack from the back of the closet where I'd stashed it, took out the newspapers, and tore them all into pieces. The reindeer watched with interest. The guinea pigs squeaked.

"It smells different in here," Cecelia said when she reappeared.

"Yeah, that's the smell of significantly less urine. You're out of kitty litter and guinea pig food."

"Oh, I'll get some more eventually."

"You'll get some more now. You know, I'm pretty sure guinea pigs are supposed to be sort of fat? How would you like it if you didn't have anything to eat for days on end?"

She shrugged. "It's not that bad."

I bit my lip. I was trying hard to stay angry, to ignore those little reminders that Cecelia was a victim, too. She didn't feed me quite consistently, and I was lucky to have a backpack half full of enchanted snacks. But I wasn't entirely sure the fairies fed her enough, either.

"And how would you feel if the toilet didn't flush, and you just had to keep pooping in it anyway, again and again, until all your poop was piled up so high you couldn't close the lid?"

"Ew."

"Exactly. Kitty litter, guinea pig food. Go get them. Now. If you can't find official food, a bunch of vegetables or something."

Cecelia nodded and darted out of the room, face a little greenish.

"You're very brave," came a soft voice from the closet. I looked back at the reindeer.

"She's just a kid. Someone has to get her in line, if her family won't."

"A kid who thinks tracing patterns in my fur with a knife tip is fun," the reindeer countered and, well. He made a good point.

"I didn't know you talked. Do the other animals, too?"

"The guinea pigs don't. Sweet animals, but not enough brains in them for making words. I don't know about the cats—some cats can, some either can't or won't admit they can. I've never heard these ones talk, but that's just smart. Cecelia doesn't know I can."

"I won't tell her," I promised.

Sometimes she was nearly sweet. She liked to talk to me about her days, though I was never quite sure whether the stories were true or not. She liked to show me all the things in her room—so much junk—and tell me where it came from. She liked to whisper to me from the top bunk late at night. And, yes, she liked to play with her little collection of knives, which occasionally involved running them through her pets' fur (never drawing blood, at least), when I couldn't stop her. I was quite certain she'd never had a friend before.

I've only ever had two friends in my life—Kai and Manda. It's not—I'm not an outcast, or anything. People don't pick on me, or not much. In middle school they did, but middle schoolers are vicious. Most of them outgrew it. But maybe I haven't quite forgiven them—maybe that's why it's hard.

I could find people to do group projects with, and to sit with at lunch—I'm good at group projects, and no one at my school is, like, send-losers-to-eat-in-the-toilets level mean, like you see on TV. I just—don't talk to them, really, and definitely don't see them outside of school.

People are hard, for me. Especially people my age; adults are easier. Though after handling all these magic people, and talking plants and animals, I'm hoping teenagers will be a little less intimidating.

Anyway, Kai and Manda. The thing is, Kai and I actually, like, fit together. We did everything together. Maybe it's just because we grew up together. Manda and I are the kinds of people who are friends with each other because we aren't—or weren't—friends with anyone else. We don't really have anything in common. And really—when we met we weren't friends with anyone else. She was new, and the teacher asked me to show her around, and we just...kept hanging out.

But the longer she was around, the more people she met that she actually fit with. And sometimes she'd invite me to do things with those people, but I always felt so awkward and out of place and, honestly, bored. We just weren't interested in any of the same things.

So I'm not really sure why Manda and I are still friends. Sometimes I think she just feels bad for me. Sometimes I think it's because I was the only person who didn't need to be told three times that it was Manda. Not Amanda. Not Mandy. Manda.

And sometimes I think it's because I'm just...always there. I'm not the person she has fun with, as much as the person she comes to with problems.

But that's not fair; she's there for me too. I talk to her about my absent parents and about Kai and—we are friends. We are. But it's never stopped me from feeling alone in the world, and I've never thought it was the kind of friendship that would last much past high school. We're friends of circumstance, not best-friend-charm, two-halves-of-a-heart friends.

And maybe that's normal. Maybe that's how normal friendships work, and maybe I'm just weirdly hung up on Kai because of nostalgia, or because I always saw him as more a brother than a friend.

I don't have a whole lot of experience with friendship, is the point. But I'm, like, ninety eight and a half percent positive it's not supposed to work like it did with Cecelia.

I was left alone often, or as alone as one could be in a small bedroom that contained an entire shelter's worth of animals. I was left without Cecelia often. I talked with the reindeer, when he felt like talking—he was unwell, I think, as well as terribly afraid of Cecelia, and what new horrors he might face if anyone else in the house realized he could speak. He did not have enough space, enough food, enough exercise. He was frightened and exhausted always, and often he did not have the energy for conversation. But when I saw that he was extra unhappy, I sat in the closet with him and stroked his head, and it seemed to make him feel a bit better.

I held the guinea pigs in my lap sometimes, and fed them carrots if there were carrots to feed them, and stroked their too-thin bodies carefully. Some would let me hold them—others were too scared, and I didn't want to upset them more than they must already be upset, just about the living situation.

I made friends with one of the cats, though not the other two—one was just very aloof, but the other was frightened and sometimes aggressive if you got too close.

I didn't bother much about the ant farms—I didn't know much about insect care, and at least one of the farms was all dead before I even arrived. Maybe two of them. It was hard to tell.

The fish were—I couldn't bond with them, exactly. And I couldn't do much to clean their tank. I tried to wipe at the thick layer of algae on the glass once with an old towel, but it had hardened down and wouldn't wipe. I thought maybe it could be scraped with a knife, but then I thought any germs on the knife might kill the fish, so better to leave things as they were. Aside from the algae on the walls, there was a lot of gunk in the water—I'm really not sure how those fish were still alive. A couple of them looked like they had fungal infections, maybe? I don't know much about fish. There was fuzzy white stuff on their fins. Some of them kept getting very fat, then thinner again, and it took me a few cycles of this to realize they were pregnant, because the other fish ate all the babies before I even noticed them.

Once I realized there were babies coming, I took a plastic cup from the bathroom, and filled it with water and let it float in the tank, then tried to gather up as many babies as I could there so that they couldn't be eaten. But it was hard work, especially with the water so filthy, and after a few tries it occurred to me that I didn't even know what I was saving them for—their quality of life was going to be absolutely terrible.

A few babies must have been successfully evading the adults in the murky water, because the number of fish seemed to keep rising, even though fish kept dying off, too. The first few times I found a dead fish floating at the top of the tank I flushed it right away, but then I thought maybe Cecelia would take more responsibility if she saw the consequences of her neglect, so I stopped.

Then there was the time I pointed out a dead fish, and she cried over it and told me its name (Susan), but absolutely refused to flush it herself. (It was too hard, she loved Susan too much, she wasn't ready.) I left it sitting there for a week, until it looked absolutely disgusting, and I was worried about its little corpse spreading diseases to the others. After that I took care of the disposal again, but I made sure to let her know whenever one died.

She cried every single time. But she wouldn't put in any work to make them stop dying.

~

I dreamt that I was running down the hall to the bathroom, the fairies chasing me, calling my name. I slammed and locked the door, but it wouldn't hold for long, not against fairies.

I looked up at the mirror, and it reflected not my face and the surrounding room, but a white winter night. I could see snow blowing across the sky.

I slammed my hands against it, certain that if I could only break the glass, I could somehow escape into that night. The glass shattered, and the shards melted like ice around my feet. A fairy pounded on the door, and I woke suddenly, back in the lower bunk in Cecelia's bedroom.

~

"How long have you been here?" I asked the reindeer one day.

"I don't know. Too long. I measure time by the comings and the goings of the snow, when I measure it at all, but I am afraid to leave my closet, and my closet has no window."

"I would promise to tell you, next time it snowed, but I'm hoping to be gone before then. I'll take you with me if I can."

"How are you planning to get away?" the reindeer asked.

"I don't know. But I will—I haven't come this far, just to give it all up for a spoiled brat who thinks this is what friendship looks like."

I had told the reindeer all about Kai. I had to talk to someone about what was going on, or I'd go mad with it. And I certainly wasn't going to be confiding in Cecelia.

The reindeer, in return, told me about the winter lands where he belonged, where he did not bother measuring time, because there was always fresh snow on the ground, and that meant the time was always right. He had not encountered the snow queen, but told me she was rumored to live in a palace at the top of the world. He told me stories of snow bees and ice foxes, and the penguins he had seen once, the farthest north he had ever gone.

At least, I think they were penguins—he called them large birds wearing fine suits.

"If you can get us both out of here," he promised me, "you will sit on my back and I will carry you deep, deep into the winter lands, where you can find your Kai."

I would get us both out. I had to. The cats and the fish and the guinea pigs—I couldn't do anything for them. Their home was terrible, but I didn't have a better one to offer. I could not carry a whole herd of little rodents into the winter lands with me, where they would only freeze to death.

~

I woke in the morning before Cecelia, as I usually did. I went to the closet first, to say good morning to the reindeer. My morning routine was to greet him, then take any dead fish with me to the bathroom, where I would brush my teeth and wash my face and get dressed, there where no one could see; Cecelia would strip in the room with no cares, but I didn't want her to see me naked, and I didn't want to hide away in the closet and inflict my nudity on the reindeer, either.

But this morning there were—so many dead fish. So many. I didn't try to count them, just scooped them all into the cup I kept by the tank for carting their little corpses around. They nearly filled the cup this time. I stirred through the water and the rocks at the bottom of the tank with the little green net to be sure—there were no living fish left. Most of the dead ones I'd scooped up had that fuzzy white stuff on their fins, or fins that were just falling apart, dissolving away.

I set the little cup of fish down on the dresser next to the tank, and went to wake Cecelia.

"Your fish are all dead," I told her; she'd killed them, with her neglect, and I didn't feel the need to sugarcoat things.

"All of them?"

"Yes."

"But—but why?"

"All of them are dead today for the same reason one of them has died every day or two since I've come here—because you take things and you don't take care of them. Because you think anything you see and like is yours to own, but you won't take any of the responsibilities of ownership. They're better off dead than they were in that little sewer you call an aquarium—all of us in this room would be better off without you, and this garbage you call love."

"It is—I do love them. You, all of you."

"Then act like. Now if you'll excuse me, I have a couple dozen fish to flush."

I left her there, and took my time in the bathroom, a little to give Cecelia some privacy after I'd said all that, but mostly because in the bathroom was the only time I was ever guaranteed to have any privacy of my own. When I came back she was crying; I ignored her and went to sit in the closet with the reindeer.

"You're not a good friend either," she said when I came out again. "You didn't even try to comfort me."

"Yeah, well, I'm not your friend. I'm a girl you kidnapped. I don't owe you anything, certainly not lies about how your behavior isn't that bad and the way you treat other living creatures isn't literally killing them."

"Why are you being so mean?"

"Because you literally kidnapped me, Cecelia!"

"I kidnapped the cats and the piggies and the reindeer too, and they're never mean to me."

"That's because they can't talk, and because they're terrified of you, and actually, the calico cat and the black and white one? Definitely mean to you. Did you think all the hissing and scratching and biting was friendly?"

She was silent for a long moment, then shouted, "Get out of my room!"

I did, gladly, but I wasn't sure where to go from there—where I would be safe from the fairies, or where the house would allow me to go—most doors wouldn't open for me. None of the outside ones, certainly. After a few minutes of uncertainty in the hallway, I went to the bathroom, locking the door behind me and sitting on the floor. I wouldn't be allowed to stay in there all day—I'd tried before—but if Cecelia was angry with me, and therefore not interested in my whereabouts, I could get away with hours, maybe, until someone else tried to use that bathroom and found I'd locked myself in. And then I would be dealing with an angry fairy, which was significantly worse than an angry Cecelia. But it was worth it, for what privacy I could get.

The bathroom was clean—the cleanest part of the house I'd encountered. None of the fairies seemed tidy, and they were certainly all hoarders, but none seemed as bad as Cecelia. I kept the bathroom clean. It was something I did for myself, not for anyone else who might use it, and since none of them seemed to care whether it was clean or not, it didn't make me feel like a maid like cleaning Cecelia's room, which I know she did care about, if not enough to do it herself. I know because she always tried to hug me when she noticed it, which I always stood stone still and endured.

The bathroom was sparkling clean, because it was my safe place in the house, and because cleaning it gave me something to do, through long, boring days. (Amazing, how bored you can be despite a frantic sense of urgency thrumming constantly beneath your skin. But I was trapped, with no way to address the urgent issue, and nothing else meaningful to do.)

I stayed in the bathroom for three blissful hours, sitting on the cool, clean tile with my back against the wall, trying not to think or worry about anything, checking my pocket watch for the time occasionally. Finally, it seemed like long enough that I shouldn't risk staying any longer, and I made my way back to the bedroom.

Cecelia was gone. I went to sit with the reindeer.

"I should dump out the aquarium while she's gone, before she tries to get more fish for it. Should probably scrub it out, too, before she inevitably starts storing random junk in there." I had no hopes of convincing her to get rid of the entire aquarium—sometimes I had to talk her into getting rid of candy bar wrappers and pencils sharpened down into tiny, unusable knubs.

"Probably the smart thing to do," agreed the reindeer.

"In a while," I said. He was sitting down, and I leaned against him. It was comfortable, despite the overcrowded chaos of the closet. I was starting to feel a little bad about what I'd said to Cecelia. But all of it had been true.

Cecelia was just like the witch in the cottage. She saw people as possessions, as things to own and control—she just wanted a friend instead of a daughter. It was good that she had me, I think. It helped put things into perspective. Because my mind was clouded when I was with the witch, and despite my best efforts, even now, I remember that time as a lovely, fairy tale sort of haze.

My mind was fully my own when I was with Cecelia, and it was horrible. Really, really awful. I was absolutely miserable the entire time. I think I would have been miserable with the witch, too, if I had been myself. I know I would have been—I was on a mission, and she derailed me. I was absolutely trapped, even if I didn't feel like it. Being with Cecelia helped me remember how dreadful the witch had really been.

I cleaned the aquarium as well as I could, and went to bed early. I laid down in my bottom bunk facing the wall, with the blankets pulled over my head. I wasn't ready to sleep, but Cecelia would be back soon, and she was a little less likely—just a little—to bother me if she thought I was asleep already.

I flipped my pocket watch open and shut idly, running first through my nightly prayers and then through my happiest memories of Kai, my reminders of why I was on the journey, and why I had to keep on going.

There was a way out of this place, and I was going to find it. I was going to find Kai, and bring him home.

~

Cecelia walked in one afternoon with a bright red handprint across her cheek—one of the fairies had hit her. Again.

"What happened?" I asked. I didn't like seeing her hurt; Cecelia wasn't a friend or even an ally, but she was certainly less an enemy than the fairies in whose house we both lived.

"Nothing. I was stupid."

"Stupid how?"

"I botched a mission. It all went wrong—we didn't steal anything, and it was all my fault."

"How was it your fault?"

"I don't know! I thought I did everything right. I was so careful!" She was near tears then, and I took her, against my better judgement, into my arms.

"It's okay. Grown-ups who hit kids are questionable already—when they also refuse to tell you exactly what you did to earn the hit, you can pretty much stop taking what they say seriously."

"I must have done something wrong. They're fairies; I'm a human. I'm the one who always messes up—they do their best to raise me right, but I'm never going to be as good as them. I'm always going to be the weak link. I told you my name as soon as we met!"

"I told you my name, too."

"Yeah, but you didn't have half a lifetime as a changeling to learn better."

I wasn't going to convince her it wasn't all her fault. Not now, when she was so worked up. And I still didn't—it was instinct, to try to comfort someone who was crying and recently slapped by a parental figure. But I didn't want—I didn't want us to be friends, and I didn't want her to think we were.

I just also didn't want her to have been hit.

~

I had, in the monotonous misery of my time there, forgotten the newspaper princess' warning to count the days. I had long since lost sense of exactly how much time had passed. But it was, if the calendar hanging on Cecelia's wall was to be believed (highly doubtful), nearly my birthday. I was coming on eighteen. And it occurred to me that half a lifetime had passed since Kai had been any better a friend to me than Cecelia was.

Well. At least he had never claimed to be.

But still. I was risking my life for someone who didn't care about me, and hadn't in years. Kai didn't deserve my love, and maybe if I loved myself a little more I wouldn't be giving it out so freely, wouldn't be sacrificing everything for someone who wouldn't so much as remember to say "Happy Birthday" to me. He only wanted to be with me when it was snowing; the only other times he ever talked to me were when he was having trouble with English homework.

And I always helped him.

I deserved better than Kai. I was wasting my life on nostalgia, unable to let go of someone who had loved me once when we were children—no wonder Manda thought I was in love with him.

(I don't know what that kind of love looks like. I know I don't...want Kai, or anyone, the way Manda and the other girls in class will talk about sometimes. I don't know what being in love is like, but I know it's not what I want with Kai. I just want my friend back. Just want my childhood back, maybe.)

I deserved better than Kai. And it wasn't wrong of me to turn him away, the last time he knocked on our wall. I didn't owe him snowy night friendship. But that was a conversation we could have later, when we were both safe at home. I was already here, in fairy land, the only one in the world who even knew he was alive, never mind where he was.

I had to save him. I couldn't live with myself if I didn't. It was about me as much as him now, and I could work out the rest when it was over.

There was a lot of time for reflection, locked up in Cecelia's bedroom. I didn't appreciate it. So far this adventure had been really heavy on the reflection, and really light on the actual adventure.

I kept thinking of Kai. I'd had three sleepovers in my life that weren't with Kai—two with Manda, which were fine, and one with a whole group of girls from school, which was nerve-wracking and miserable. Every other night of my life, as far as I could remember, that hadn't been spent in a hotel or in my own bedroom, had been spent in Kai's or on the pullout couch downstairs.

Nights in a bunk bed meant nights with Kai, whispers in the dark and grand plans for what we'd do in the morning. I didn't want Cecelia's whispers in the dark, primarily because she'd kidnapped me, but also because she wasn't him.

It began to be painful. I didn't want, anymore, to think of Kai when I was trapped with Cecelia. I didn't want to think of how, like her, he only came to me when he wanted something, or how, like her, he took whatever I gave and never offered anything in return, or how, like her, he was an absolutely garbage friend.

I didn't want to think of his crooked smile before he got braces, back when he was always smiling. I didn't want to think of the time he told me that—or the time he called me—I didn't want to think of the good times, or the bad ones, didn't want to think of him at all.

Which was ridiculous, because I was here to rescue him—how could I not think of him?

But sitting in Cecelia's bottom bunk felt exactly like standing in silence at the bus stop with Kai. It felt like being all alone in the world even though there was another person right there. It felt like being homesick in your own bedroom.

I didn't just want Kai back. I wanted my Kai back. But living in a crammed room with a garbage friend was a constant reminder that my Kai didn't exist anymore.

Maybe he never did. Maybe I made him who I needed him to be in my memory, when I was twelve years old and alone in the world, and I needed to convince myself that it hadn't always been that way, that someone had really loved me once.

No. No, I knew Kai. He was my best friend once, and I was his. I didn't imagine that, didn't make it up and convince myself it was true, the way Cecelia was doing with this thing she called a friendship.

Kai had loved me, once. And I still loved him.

Just, sometimes I wished I didn't. I stopped my nighttime reminiscing. I mentioned Kai in my daily prayers, and otherwise tried not to think too hard about him.

But winter was not far away. And I had a time limit—the third week in January, the newspaper princess had said, and I had no real idea anymore what day it was.

I lost my temper. Cecelia mentioned, offhandedly, as she often did, how nice it was that she had a friend now, who would never, ever leave her.

"You don't get to just keep people! I'm not one of those stupid trinkets on your shelf, and I don't belong to you. And we will never, never be friends, because you have no idea what friendship even is. You don't see me. You don't know me, and you don't want to. You have a person-shaped void in your life, and you thought you could grab any person off the street to fill it, and just alter them to suit your needs. I will never be what you want, so just get a stuffed animal or something and let me leave."

She stared at me, wide eyed, for a long, awful moment. Finally, she said, "It's not as if you have anywhere better to be. You were all alone, when we found you."

"I was on my way somewhere. To find someone. To save him. I came all the way from—from Minnesota, into fairy land, to rescue him from the snow queen, and you—you stopped me."

"Why do you want to save him?" Cecelia asked.

"Because I love him."

"And you think if you save him, he'll love you back?"

"No. No, I don't—want anything from him. I just want to know he's okay. I just want him to be—I just don't want to live in a world without him in it."

"Oh."

"Love isn't owning people, Cecelia."

"Oh," she said again.

"And if I don't find him in time, he might—I can't be too late."

"You have to find him," she said quietly. "You have to save him. Like—like a story in a book."

"Yes."

"I'll—I'll make the back door open for you."

"And the reindeer," I said, knowing I was pushing it. "It isn't fair, keeping him in your closet—he belongs out in the snow somewhere. He'll die here, like the ants and the fish."

"And the reindeer," she echoed.

I turned away from her, collecting my things in a hurry. This wouldn't last. She could change her mind at any moment, and even if she didn't, there was her family. I couldn't push things any further—my sleigh was lost, and all of my supplies. I had my pocket watch, and the blue dress and red boots I'd gotten from the witch in the cottage. Grandma's hat. The backpack I'd saved from the sleigh, empty now. It was too bad, leaving the pants and sweaters behind, especially, but I had no idea where they were.

My cloak was hanging in the reindeer's closet. I would take that, at least—I was headed for the winter lands, and I couldn't survive without it. I took it off the hanger and swung it over my shoulders, and Cecelia didn't stop me. I saw a pair of mittens sitting on the floor, and grabbed those too—I would need them more than she would—then I led the reindeer out of the closet and out of the room.

At the last moment I turned back; Cecelia was standing where I'd left her, and she was crying, silently, tears streaming down her face.

It wasn't fair. She was just a kid, a human kid like me, trapped too long in fairy land and morphed by it, but still not a fairy, and I knew how alone she felt. I knew exactly how she felt. It wasn't fair.

She deserved better. She deserved a real chance at a real life. But it wasn't my job to give it to her. She'd treated me badly, however bad her own life was, and I didn't owe her anything just because we were both lonely little girls, outsiders in our own homes. I already had a crappy friend to rescue.

The halls didn't twist away from me this time. I walked down a flight of stairs and straight out the back door, and then I mounted the reindeer—with some difficulty—and he ran us out of the city. Due north, according to my compass, though he didn't have to consult it at all. The winter called to him. Neither of us spoke at all until we were outside the city gates.

Chapter 11

We paused to rest when the fairy city was a speck in the distance. I slid clumsily off the reindeer's back, and sat on the ground, despite the thin layer of snow there.

"We've done it. We're free."

"And all it took was shouting at her," the reindeer said.

"I've shouted at her plenty—I just shouted the right things this time, I guess."

I slipped off my backpack and checked the various pockets for any bits of food I might have missed—no luck. And I thought I would be too afraid, now, to ask anyone else we met for food. No berries to pick, either, with snow on the ground.

It didn't matter. We'd escaped Cecelia, and we would rescue Kai. We would.

"I suppose we'd better keep moving."

The reindeer nodded. "I will take you to the gates of the snow queen's palace, but no farther, for I am not a brave beast."

"That will be plenty far; thank you."

It was easier to climb onto his back, the second time. I felt a pang of regret for the sleigh the newspaper princess had given me, which had never even reached the environment it was meant for. But the reindeer, I learned quickly, was better, at least for speed.

He ran, I think, faster than any car I've ever been in. He ran through the night and into the next day with no food or rest. I think I might have fallen asleep for a bit, on his back, but he didn't let me fall.

It was beginning to be proper winter, out here, as it hadn't been yet in the city. Everything was white, as far as I could see, the ground and the sky and everything between. It was snowing—indeed, it hardly stopped snowing for a moment, all that winter.

"We're on the ice now," the reindeer paused to tell me, and on and on and on we ran.

He stopped suddenly, after some time, and I nearly went flying over his head. When I had settled myself, I saw that we had stopped to avoid running right into an ice house. It looked just like the fishing houses people set up on the lakes through the winter at home.

"Come in, come in," cried a hoarse, cheerful voice from inside, and a moment later the door popped open, and a woman leaned out. She was tall and tan with short, light hair, and was dressed more like a modern human than most people I'd seen in fairy land.

"Come in," she said again, "both of you, and let me make you some dinner. You have a hungry look about you, and I'm past due for houseguests—no one quests north anymore."

The reindeer and I were both shy—sensibly, I thought—of strangers, but she seemed friendly, and I was hungry, and I felt instinctively, like I had with the newspaper princess, that I could trust her. I dismounted, and approached with caution, the reindeer following. We knew nothing about the snow queen, really; it would be smart to spend time with someone who might answer our questions. She was the first person we'd seen since the snow began to fall.

When she turned her back to us, I saw she had a tail like a donkey's or a cow's, the main part of it just the same color as her skin, and the little tuft of fur at the end matching her hair.

I was surprised to find that we all fit easily into the ice house, though I suppose I shouldn't have been, after all the magic I'd been exposed to by then. It was much bigger on the inside. She had about a dozen perfect circles carved into the ice, each with a fishing line sitting in it; the poles were in buckets beside the holes.

There was a long bench at the back of the house, with a little gas stove sitting on the end, and a few stools and space heaters scattered about. I wondered if they were real space heaters, or just something magic she'd made to look like them, and then decided it probably didn't matter much.

"Sit, sit," she said, "and I'll heat up the stove. What brings you so far north?"

"I'm going to rescue my friend from the snow queen."

"Oh, a proper quest then. It's been such a long time. Tell me all about it, and by the time you're done, the food will be, too."

I told her as much as I dared—I'd learned, by then, to leave out important details like people's names. Soon the food was ready—fried fish on a little metal plate.

"Don't you need to eat, too?" I asked the reindeer.

"Not here," he said. "I am a magical creature, and here in my home I can feed on the cold, though in the city I must eat like you and everyone."

"Can you tell me what I will be facing?" I asked when I'd eaten. "With the snow queen?"

"Oh, no one rightly knows. A mystery, that one. Some say she's the North Wind's daughter, and some say she's his bride. There are those who say she's just a troll that got uppity, but it's been a hundred lifetimes since a troll drew enough magic for half the feats the snow queen's accomplished. All anyone really knows is that she lives in a palace of ice at the top of the world. You've a long journey yet to reach it. But reindeer have the fleetest feet in all of fairy land, and when winter comes to the winter lands, the hours fly like birds."

She turned away from me, pulling another fish out of the large cooler that was sitting near the bench. She fried it, and when she was done she pulled a pen out of her pocket, which must have been enchanted, for she used it to write a small paragraph on the fried fish, in a language I didn't recognize. When she was done with that, she wrapped the fish in paper and set it in a much smaller blue cooler, which she handed to me.

"Here. If you continue north, you will meet my neighbor. You must give her this message for me, and she will be a good host to you. Now. You'd best be moving—it's a long way you have to go, and I have fish to catch."

So we left the ice house, and I climbed back up onto the reindeer. We rode on and on and on, the cooler in my lap, and I pulled out the pocket watch, and saw the clock's hands were spinning wildly. The hours fly like birds, the ice fisher had said—was this what she meant? I watched the sun rise, and set, and rise again, and then move backwards through the sky to set again on the wrong side of the world. I had no real sense of the passage of time, except that it felt more like hours than days. The reindeer ran, and we did not speak to each other, and did not pause for food or drink or sleep. It felt like a dream; it felt like it had just begun and like it would never end. I held the handle of the cooler with one hand, and the reindeer's neck with the other, and thought of Kai, in a palace at the top of the world.

How far away could the top of the world be? Was fairy land in the same world as Minnesota? It must be a thousand-thousand miles from my hometown to the north pole. But everything here was magic, and the reindeer was very fast.

At last we came to the place the ice fisher had sent us to. It was not what I expected. It looked like nothing so much as a very large, squat chimney, with smoke billowing furiously out the top. It gave off a warm, tropical heat, and the snow was melted for several feet around its base in all directions.

I slipped off the reindeer's back, and took a step toward the chimney, out of the snow and into the radius of its warmth. It was like a summer day, and when I reached out to touch the wall with the hand not holding the cooler, it was like touching a space heater. I turned back to look at the reindeer.

"Are you coming?"

"Oh, no, the warmth is not for me—I have lots of ice to absorb still before I'm back to my old self. But I'll be waiting right here when you're through."

He stepped back into the snow, and I knocked on the little wooden door that broke up the rough rocks of the chimney.

A little old woman opened it, tiny and hunched over, with snow white hair. She was wearing what I recognized as a bunad, from Grandma's one ancient photo of her own grandmother, still in Norway. She smiled brightly and ushered me it.

"Oh, a visitor; how lovely! And I see you've brought a gift from my friend on the ice."

I handed her the cooler, and she set it on the tiny wooden countertop next to the stove to open. She took the fish out and read the message, then laughed and shook her head. "Fish mail. If you must have neighbors, child, have neighbors that will make you laugh." She set the fish down, and searched a cupboard above her head for a frying pan. "Come, sit, sit; I will turn your letter into dinner. And what might your name be, my dear?"

"I don't mean to be rude, but I've learned not to answer that question in fairy land."

"Oh, no fear of that—I'm human. But of course, you needn't tell me anything you don't want to—I was only making conversation. And indeed, I couldn't answer the question myself—I've quite forgotten my own name over the years. It seems memory loss is the best defense against wicked fairies."

"How did you come to live in fairy land, if you're a human?"

"My dear departed husband—God rest his soul—my husband died young, and the next winter I stumbled and fell through the world. I landed here, and here I have stayed, for there were no children yet, nor anything else to keep me there." She sighed. "Perhaps I'm not quite as human as once I was; it's true that time changes all things. Still, I'm the most human creature you'll find in the winter lands, unless you're after that boy the snow queen herself brought through."

"I am. That's why—I've crossed fairy land to find him."

"And who might he be to you? No, no, don't answer me—I love to guess these sorts of things. I think, oh, not a lover, certainly. You don't have that look about you. A brother. Yes, he must be your brother."

"Well—"

"Oh, sibling love is a powerful thing, dear, a powerful thing. My husband—God rest his soul—my husband used to tell me the story of a woman who held her tongue for a dozen years, and sewed a dozen shirts of nettles, to free her brothers from enchantment."

Grandma used to tell me a story like that, too. "He's not really my brother," I told the woman.

"No? But he's the brother of your heart, darling, that I can see clearly, and love doesn't run on blood."

She finished reheating the fish, and set two little plates and two little forks on the tiny table I was sitting at. We ate the fish together.

"You must not linger here," she told me when we were done. "Your friend has been in the palace of ice for too long, already—this is not a cold for mortals to dwell in. I live here under an enchantment provided long ago by a friend, and I know I would not survive without it. But stop here with your brother on the journey back, when you have time to rest a little. And I will send you with the cooler to return to my neighbor." She stood up. "Now, then. Pretty young things like you often make the mistake of thinking lovers have all the magic. But true love is true love, child, and don't you forget it. You have all the power you need inside your own heart. Besides, the snow queen is nothing so scary—just a great, blustery bit of wind." She leaned forward and took my hands, and pressed a soft kiss to my forehead. "Good luck, my dear, and may God and all his angels ride with you."

I stepped back outside, warm and fed and somehow less tired than I had been, though I still had not slept in days, at least. The reindeer was waiting for me just where I'd left him, where the snow transitioned abruptly into fresh green grass.

"Ready, then?" he asked.

"Ready," I said, and I redid the clasp of my cloak, and climbed onto his back.

We rode on and on and on, the sun and moon flying across the sky even more quickly than the reindeer could run. He slowed, at last, when the wind came at us with such great force I thought for a moment it would drive us back, would send us flying all the way back into the little chimney house.

But the reindeer went on, undaunted, though each step was a battle, and the snow flew at our faces like missiles. And at last there was something tall and glistening in the distance, and when the snow cleared for a moment we could see that it was a castle.

The reindeer forged ahead a little farther, and farther, and farther still, until at last the palace was no more than a hundred yards away. He slowed to a stop, and I took the hint and dismounted; he could take me no farther.

"I must go, Gerda, I must fly." He leant forward to press his soft, warm nose into my cheek, and then he turned and ran, disappearing quickly into the heavy falling snow, and I was alone.

In front of me was a great palace of ice, and behind me was nothing but an endless expanse of snow. Forward, then—where else but in an ice palace could I expect to find a snow queen? And where else but with the snow queen could I expect to find Kai?

Still, I hesitated, though the cold was biting and painful, and each snowflake that landed on my skin felt like a prick from a needle.

I was afraid. Kai was inside, but Kai had been there for nearly a year, and was enchanted, and wasn't likely to listen to anything I had to say even when he wasn't enchanted. It would be good to have a friend, going in. I wished the reindeer had stayed.

The snowfall lessened, and the wind died down, and still I stood before the icy gates.

I remembered suddenly what the bee had told me about snowflakes, at the wild rose bush, long ago, now, long, long ago. I squinted at the snow, studying it carefully, and decided that he was half right, at least. Most of the snow fell steadily downward from the sky, and when I reached out a hand to catch it on my mitten, it melted into water drops, as snow was wont to do.

But some of the snow flew horizontally, or back and forth and around in dizzying patterns. And the more I looked, the more it seemed as if these were slightly larger specks in the sky. Those snowflakes, I thought, were not made of water, but were the snow bees that the bumble bee had told me of. I picked one out in the sky, following its pattern for a while, and when the moment was right, I reached out and caught it in my mitten, and drew it toward my face.

"Don't be afraid! Hello! I was hoping that you could help me."

The snow bee—and I could see, at this distance, that it was a bee, just exactly like a bumble bee, round and fuzzy and charming, but all in a perfect white, from antennas to toes, with clear glass wings—the snow bee made a low buzzing sound, and its antennas twitched.

"What do you need help with?"

"I'm searching for the snow queen," I said, impulsively. Surely it would be better to sneak in and smuggle Kai out, as I had planned to do when I thought he was with the newspaper princess. But it seemed, in the moment, like the right thing to say.

"Oh, you needn't worry about that," the snow bee buzzed. "We are all precious to her, and as soon as I touched your hand, she began gathering herself to greet you. She will be here soon, quite soon."

The bee flew immediately away, and I quickly lost sight of him as the wind began to rise again. It blew furiously around me for some time, then settled slowly into the shape of a woman, lovely and strange.

"What are you?" she asked, in quite a normal, human-sounding voice, just a little echoey. "Why have you come to my home, and why have you bothered my bees?"

"I'm a human girl, and I'm here for my friend."

"There are no friends for you here, child."

"I'm here for the boy you took last winter."

"Oh, yes. I did not think he would have any friends."

So she'd gotten to know him a bit, then. "What are you?" I asked, since she'd asked first, and since it seemed to be something of a mystery.

"I am the wind," she said. "I am the snow, the ice. I am Winter."

"You took him."

"No," she said. "I accepted him. He came to me."

"He didn't mean to. He didn't know."

"Tell him, then. Take him back."

"And you'll let me? Just like that?" After all I'd gone through to get here, we weren't even going to fight about it? Not that I minded.

"And how would I stop you? I am nothing, just the cold."

I studied her for a moment. "You're lonely."

There was a long moment of quiet, during which I tried and failed to make out the expression on her wind-blown, ever-changing face. "I suppose I am," she said slowly, as if the idea had never occurred to her. "I fought with the North Wind. He drove out the trolls to spite me, blew them far, far away where I could never find them, and he told everyone else that I was a wild, wicked thing." She sighed, a soft, blustery sound. "I am wild. But not wicked—I'm just cold."

I was reminded, suddenly, of the many times someone in school had called me an ice princess. Usually because I didn't visibly react to something mean that someone—usually Kai—said. Sometimes because I refused to put up with what was allegedly flirting.

She was lonely because people thought she didn't have feelings, or at least not the right ones. My feelings never seemed to be the right ones—if I endured jerks I was an unfeeling robot, and if I shut them down I was frigid.

"I've seen trolls," I offered, and suddenly all the wind went completely still.

"Where?" she asked, quiet and breathless.

"On the other side of the forest of time, south of the mountain range."

The wind began to pick up again, moving here and there in frantic little flurries. "Oh! Oh, I must go. I must find them, while the southern lands are still frozen and cold. Oh, my poor darlings— they're not meant for such a climate. The sunny days—"

"What about Kai?"

"You may take him back if you can, but I am not convinced he is suited for human lands. There is ice in his heart, and I am not the one who put it there. I didn't think he was human at first, he was so cold inside. I thought maybe he was a troll. Or a snowman. It's been some time since I saw a snowman walking about." She sighed. "But then, perhaps he is not suited for my lands, either. I cannot return him home myself; he's grown too hot to touch. I melted a finger on him, the last time I tried."

"I will get him home. Just tell me, please, where to find him?"

"Oh, he's somewhere about the place. The ballroom, perhaps? I gave him a puzzle to do. Children like puzzles, don't they?"

"Where is—"

"I must go—my trolls are waiting! You may take the boy, and whatever you like from the palace, but I haven't the time—it's been lifetimes since they've been safe at home."

The figure of a woman dissolved into the blowing snow, and I was alone. I did hope she would find the trolls, and they would want to come home with her, but I wished she'd stayed long enough to take me to Kai, and maybe to give us some advice on getting out of here. (Should I be worried that he was too hot for her to touch? And who had put ice in his heart? I was pretty sure she didn't just mean he was a jerk.)

The gates to the palace were wide open, and so I walked in. It had many very tall towers, but I thought a ballroom would probably be on the ground floor. Likely near the main entrance as well, since it would be primarily for hosting guests, and you wouldn't want them to have to wander all through your house to get there.

At least, that's how I imagined it would be in a logically laid out mansion, but we were in fairy land, and it didn't seem like the snow queen had been hosting a lot of guests—it sounded like before she found Kai, it had been her and the snow bees alone for a long, long time.

I did hope she brought the trolls home.

The inside of the palace was a little warmer than the outside, since it was protected from the wind, but it was made all of ice, so it was still quite cold. I decided to walk through in as near a straight line as possible, first—I didn't want to get lost in a maze of frozen castle hallways.

It felt like I'd been walking for years by the time I stumbled into a large, open room with a small figure sitting in the center of it, in front of a little pile of ice shards. But time had felt strange since nearly the moment we entered the winter lands—that didn't mean anything anymore.

I ran to Kai, boots slipping on the icy floor, and he didn't look up at me until I was nearly on top of him.

His eyes were bloodshot, wild and unfocused. (Of course they were unfocused; he wasn't wearing his glasses, and he's as blind as a bat.) For one moment we made eye contact, a fraction of a second before Kai's gaze went skittering away, with no recognition or acknowledgement.

I knelt on the ground beside him and tugged off my mitten before touching his arm—burning hot in all this snow, feverish, and that explained the eyes, too.

"Go away, Gerda," he mumbled, not looking at me. "You suck at puzzles."

"Kai."

"Go away," he repeats. "Just go—I'm so sick of this." His fevered gaze met mine again, with an expression I couldn't quite read, but I knew I didn't like it.

"You've been hallucinating," I guessed. His temperature seemed high enough for it.

"Yeah, wish I could hallucinate someone useful for once."

His refusal to look at me made more sense now, and I cupped his face in my hands, though it did nothing to stop the frantic motion of his eyes.

"Kai. I'm real."

"Nothing's real," he mumbled, trying to pull away. "It's all a fairy tale here. A bad one."

"Fairy tale. All right." I leant forward slowly, and dropped the gentlest of kisses on his burning, desert-dry lips. "There. True love's kiss. All better."

"You don't love me," he said. But he took a deep, shuddering breath, and tears were rising in his eyes. I pulled him into my arms, half into my lap, and held him close to my chest.

"Of course I do, Kai. Of course."

We wept together, tears forming a warm pool that began to melt the icy ground. He cried, my Kai, my Kai again, long after my eyes were dry.

"Kai," I said when he finally seemed done, "Kai, it's all right."

He looked up at me, eyes still bloodshot, but not so wild. His gaze seemed clearer, more focused, than I'd expect with the glasses still missing.

"Tell me what's happened?" I asked.

He gestured at the shards of glass on the floor. "I have to spell eternity."

"Why?"

Kai ignored the question, reaching up to touch his eyes. "Gerda."

"What?"

"Gerda, I can see."

"What?"

"Really seeing. Like it's the middle of the night and I've come to find you in the snow. I mean, everything's still blurry, but I feel like I can see. Gerda."

I began to laugh, not quite sure why. After a moment of confusion he joined in, the sound soft and hesitant, utterly unlike his school laugh. I couldn't remember the last time I heard him laugh at home.

"It worked, Kai. True love's kiss. It worked."

"We're not in love," he pointed out when we were both calm again.

"Different kinds of love, Kai. Just like a boy, always thinking about sex." I grinned at him like I hadn't since elementary school.

We sat there, thinking, for a few more minutes. I didn't really understand what had happened, and I doubted Kai did either, and I didn't know how to ask. He seemed—seemed like my Kai again.

Staring at the ground, I noticed something I could swear hadn't been there before—two tiny shards of glass, or maybe ice, just at our feet.

"Kai. Your puzzle!" I scooped the fragments up and dropped them carefully in his palm. "You were just missing some pieces."

The word fell into place with a sound like bells—eternity, a jagged, glistening word against the snow.

"Come home, Kai," I said. "Come home."

"I don't know how."

"I'll help you."

"I don't know who I am now. I feel like I've been under a spell."

"I think you have been." There was ice in his heart, and the snow queen didn't put it there. And then there was extra ice on the ground. "Come home, Kai. Your grandmother is waiting, and we have a long way to go still."

"All right. Let's go home. I'm freezing."

We stood up, and turned around, and sitting on the ground behind us, where they definitely hadn't been before, were the snow things Kai had left home wearing—coat and snow pants, one winter boot, hat and scarf and one glove. I recognized the scarf, especially—Grandma had made it for him.

Sitting a few feet away were another boot and another glove, in completely different, much older-fashioned styles, to make up for the ones he'd lost on the hill at home. I decided I didn't want to know where the snow queen had gotten them.

"Well, get dressed then. Always wandering around in t-shirts in the winter; you're ridiculous."

"Yeah, well, I've never been cold like this before. I wasn't, just before you came. And speaking of ridiculous—what on earth are you wearing?"

I looked down at myself—the velvet cloak, the blue dress, the red boots, and of course, Grandma's hat. I'd been wearing this for so long now, it felt normal. "The cloak was a gift from a newspaper fairy. The rest I got from the first person who kidnapped me."

"A newspaper fai—wait, first person?"

"Yep. We have three kidnappings between the two of us now. That's gotta be some kind of record—we can check with Guinness when we get home."

"I don't think they accept submissions from delusional teens claiming to have stumbled out of a fairy tale," he said.

"Maybe not." He was dressed for the weather by then, and I took his gloved hand and pulled him toward the hallway— whatever he'd said about really seeing, he was clearly still working blind.

We'd been walking through the hallway in silence for a while before we stumbled upon another pile of things that definitely hadn't been there the last time I came through. I reached down to pick up a delicate little globe made of glass, and handed it carefully to Kai, then picked up the pair of ice skates in the exact same shade of red as my boots. I showed them to Kai, holding them close to his face since I wasn't sure exactly how bad his eyes had gotten, over the years, and he started to laugh.

He laughed for a long time, sounding increasing hysterical, and I took back the globe so he wouldn't drop it. I didn't do anything else—he'd been through a lot, and maybe it would be good to get whatever this was out of his system before we went out into the blizzard.

"What is it?" I asked when he'd calmed down a little.

"The whole world and a new pair of skates. She promised me the whole world and a new pair of skates if I could spell eternity."

"But Kai, you hate ice skating."

"I know."

"It's a beautiful little world she's given you, though."

"I feel like—like I got the whole world back. Not some pretty little trinket. You came, and we cried, and you found those last two puzzle pieces, and I feel—I feel like the world is real again. Like I was on the wrong side of the glass for a long time, and someone let me back inside."

"I wish we had something to keep this stuff in, though. The skates can go in my bag. But the globe would get jostled and break."

Kai shrugged. I turned around, and was not exactly surprised to find a backpack sitting on the floor, empty except for a long strip of velvet that worked quite nicely to wrap up the fragile globe. Kai pulled on the loaded backpack, and we were on our way again.

It was a long walk. Kai seemed dazed and distracted. When the door I'd come in through was not too far away, he stopped abruptly and asked, "Why did you come?"

"Because I love you, doofus. I know you. I knew you weren't dead, and a boy like you, Kai—you're either dead or in trouble."

"Thanks."

"You're my friend, Kai. Of course I came."

"And you're sure you're not a hallucination?"

I grabbed his hand again. "Super sure. Let's go home."

Chapter 12

It wasn't until we stepped out of the palace that I realized what an impossible journey we had ahead of us. It had taken the reindeer immeasurable days, fueled by magic, to cross the winter lands. Kai and I could only walk. I had eaten last I didn't know how long ago, and had slept far longer ago than that. I didn't know how long it had been for Kai, but I thought it was too long; he hadn't looked well when I found him, and looked little better now.

We both gasped as the icy air hit our faces, but there was only one way out of this place. I took a breath, and took a step forward, and Kai followed.

By the time we had walked a hundred yards—or my best estimate at it—I knew we could not survive without the reindeer's magic. I was holding Kai's hand tight in my own; we could not afford to be separated in a raging snowstorm, and I knew he could hardly see, though my sight was little better in this weather. It was painfully cold, and I was exhausted already. But when I turned back toward the palace, I couldn't see it.

It didn't matter. We couldn't have gone back. I do not believe the snow queen was evil, but we could not have survived in her home any more than we could have standing naked in the blizzard. Or at least, I couldn't, and since he'd lost the shards of glass in his heart, I suspected Kai could not either.

We each took another step forward, and another; we were equally blinded by the force of the snowfall, and I was not at all certain we were moving in the right direction. I was only hoping that, if we were truly at the top of the world, south was all directions, and if we did not reach the part of the world we sought, we would at least still reach a part where it was warmer.

I took another step, and banged into something warm and solid and soft. I reached forward with my free hand, fumbling until I found a familiar antler, a familiar nose.

"Reindeer? You waited for me?"

"I am not ready yet to face the snow queen, but I could not let you die in the cold for my fear. Besides, I am very good at waiting."

"Thank you, reindeer," I said, and threw my free hand around his neck.

"Come, get onto my back, you and your friend both. You can neither of you take much more of this cold."

"You are strong enough for both of us?"

"I am," he said, and so I climbed on, and pulled Kai up behind me.

I wrapped my arms around the reindeer's neck, and Kai wrapped his arms around my waist, and leaned forward to whisper in my ear, "Are we riding a talking reindeer?"

"Yeah."

"Does he fly, too?"

"No, but he runs so fast he might as well."

"Cool."

"Yeah," I agreed. "It really is." All the magic of fairy land seemed somehow more magical, with Kai at my side.

We rode on and on and on, and we did not talk, though I longed to; the wind was rushing too quickly past our ears. We came at last to the little chimney house, and slid off the reindeer's back, cold and stiff and aching.

"We will rest here," I told Kai, "and eat a little."

He nodded. He looked rather dazed and far-off, though that might just have been an effect of his partial blindness.

I knocked on the door, and the old woman opened it right away. "Oh, you're back! I did so hope you would be. A successful mission, I take it?"

She tilted her chin toward Kai, standing behind me, and I nodded.

"Good, good. Well, come in out of the cold, both of you."

We sat across from each other at the little wooden table while she worked at the stove. Kai was uncharacteristically quiet, and shaking despite a warmth that was almost uncomfortable.

"Are you okay?" I asked, and he nodded.

"It's been a fair amount of trauma, I'd imagine," said the old woman without turning to face us. "It'll take the boy some time to adjust, to heal. The soup is nearly done, and then you need a good long rest, both of you. It will all be better when you wake up, at least a little. It always is."

When we had eaten, the old woman unfolded two beds from the wall, and Kai and I curled up in one together without discussion; he was still shaking, and I remembered suddenly that it wasn't just the cold outside affecting him—he'd been feverish when I found him.

I woke some time later; Kai was still asleep beside me, burning, burning hot.

There was a fire in the fireplace, casting a warm glow across the entire room, and I saw the old woman asleep in the second bed she'd pulled out. I walked toward her, then hesitated, not sure if I should wake her, if it was fair to ask her to help me with this, when she had already opened her home to us, fed us, and given us a bed to sleep in.

She woke, herself, before I could come to a decision, and sat up in her bed. "Something is wrong."

"Kai is sick," I told her, before remembering I wasn't supposed to give out names in fairy land.

"I'm Gerda," I added, to make things even. I did trust her. But Kai's name hadn't been mine to share. (He had only been with the snow queen, all this time I'd been travelling; I would have to make sure he knew to hold his name close.)

The woman laid a hand on Kai's forehead, and frowned. "There's a tin pail sitting by the door. Go and fill it with snow. We need to break the fever."

I did, just barely remembering to slip my boots back on before running outside.

The reindeer was standing just at the border where the warm green ground turned back to snow, and he looked up when I came out. "Are we leaving so soon?"

"No—we'll be staying longer than expected, I think. K—he's sick."

The reindeer nodded. "I thought he felt a bit warm on my back, but then I thought, what do I know of human body temperatures?"

"We can't leave again until he's better—I'm sorry."

"I'm happy here, Gerda—go help your friend."

Kai was mostly asleep, and occasionally delirious, for what felt like three days, though I was sure if we were outside, watching the rapid passage of the sun, it would have proven to be much longer. The old woman hardly let me near him in that time.

"I have been steeped in magic since your grandmother's grandmother was a child; I'm far past being stricken down by a pneumonia or an influenza. You, my dear, are not, and I do not need two sick children to care for."

So I carried out the needed household tasks, the way the witch in the cottage had taught me in my delirious first few months in fairy land. I prepared food from the little enchanted store room the woman showed me, and washed my clothes and Kai's, both for the first time in many months. I checked on the reindeer, and tended the little garden behind the chimney house, and swept and mopped. Kai stayed in his bed, and the chimney woman and I took turns sleeping in the other. I did not think either of us kept very regular hours, but it was impossible to tell, in this winter land where the sun came and went as it pleased.

Finally, I walked in from the outside to hear her saying, "Here, sit up a little; your sister's just coming in."

"My sis—oh, you mean Gerda." His voice was hoarse, but not vague and confused like it had been the last few times I'd heard it.

"Feeling better?" I asked him.

"Yeah. Um. Sort of confused. But better."

"Good." I came to sit beside him on the bed, and the old woman didn't try to shoo me away, so she must have thought the danger of contagion was past. "I know you were already kind of sick when I found you—do you remember everything about the snow queen? About leaving?"

"Yeah. At least, I think so? Was there really a talking reindeer?"

"There was. He's outside right now. He's been worried about you."

"This place is so weird."

"Yeah, kinda grows on you, though."

He looked skeptical.

He looked like Kai.

"All right," the woman said. "Dinner, then it's back to bed for you, young man; rest is the best cure for all ailments."

We ate, and we slept, and ate again—breakfast, sweet, paper-thin pancakes with cherries and syrup—and the old woman went out into the yard, and left us alone.

I sat beside Kai on the little bed in the little chimney house, with its warm, dull light, and it was the first time we had been together, just the two of us with nothing terrifying hanging over our heads, since we'd sat on our swing under the falling snow, a few weeks before we'd both left home. The bed was small, and we were pressed tightly together the way we used to be in our snow forts, warm and together despite the winter all around us.

We sat in silence for a while—I wasn't quite sure who Kai was anymore, how to talk to him, and I suppose he felt the same way about me. It had been years since he'd seemed really unsure of himself, but he did now, had since I'd found him.

After some time the silence began to shift from comfortable to awkward. And I knew the woman had gone outside to give us some time alone, and it seemed we should make some use of it.

"What did you mean," I asked him, "when you said you could really see?"

He sighed. "It's not, like, the actual vision thing—I really miss my glasses. Just, for a really long time, everything has looked sort of—ugly and awful and...sort of dull? And wrong. Like—like seeing life through a shower door. And—and I cried—I can't remember the last time I cried—and all of the sudden the whole world looks like a place worth living in again."

"Is that why you—why you got so...different?"

"Mean?" he asked.

"Well. Yeah."

"Yeah," he echoed. "I guess it was."

"I missed you. You got mean, and you left me behind, and I missed you so much."

He turned around, with difficulty, in the narrow space we had to navigate. "I never left you. I sucked, but I didn't leave you. I mean, until I came here, but that was—you didn't mean now."

"You did. You grew up mean, and I was all alone in the world."

"I grew up mean. But I didn't leave. I—I pushed you away, but I didn't leave. You're the one who moved from the bunk bed to the pullout couch, you're the one who stopped coming over when your parents didn't leave you there, and you're the one who started coming again just to hang out with my grandma."

"You stopped picking up the tin can phone. And you always said no when Grandma and I asked you to do stuff with us."

"Yeah," he said quietly. "I did. I cut the string on the phone. I knew—I knew you didn't like me anymore. I just didn't want to keep—to keep trying to pretend."

"Oh. I—I'm sorry."

"I was being awful—stopping hanging out with me was the right thing to do."

"I stopped hanging out with you because I didn't think you liked me anymore! Now I feel like I abandoned you."

He shrugged. "Everything...everything still feels weird, but I'm pretty sure I deserved abandoning."

"No one deserves abandoning," I said, and then I thought of Cecelia, who I'd abandoned, and the witch, who I'd also kind of abandoned, and, okay, maybe some people deserved abandoning. But not Kai. (And maybe I'd technically abandoned everyone at home, but that was an accident—I didn't mean to wander into fairy land.)

"I was trying to apologize, not guilt-trip you," he said, frustrated just like he gets when I don't understand my math homework.

I shrugged. I knew he wasn't trying to guilt trip me, but I still felt guilty.

He sighed. "Fine. We abandoned each other. Whatever. I think we both need to forgive ourselves and each other for what we did when we were kids. The stuff I said a couple weeks ago, you can still be mad about."

"A couple—Kai, it's been a year."

"What?"

"Well, it was eight months last time I was really sure of the date, and maybe nine or ten on the less trustworthy calendar, but that was—I think that was a really long time ago. Things don't happen...normally, here. You disappeared last January. I came right after you, but I got stuck a few times, and I went through this time forest—it's next winter. It's been—you thought it had been a few weeks?"

"I thought—I don't know. It felt like a very, very long time. Like years. But it also felt like no time at all. Every—everyone must think we're dead."

"They've thought you were dead since the Monday after you left; some of your stuff washed up from the river."

"That's—you left Grandma alone, when she already thought I was dead?"

"I—I had to find you. I didn't expect it to take so long."

"You should have left it alone. You should have stayed with her."

"And let her go on thinking you were dead forever?"

"Yes! Of course. I'm—I'm an awful grandson; she may be better off without me, but even if she's not—the two of us are all she has. And you made her lose both of us? You left her all alone?"

"I'm bringing you back to her. I'm bringing us both back."

"You never should have left. I don't—how could you do such a stupid—"

"Hey! I have crossed worlds to rescue you, Kai; the least you could do is be nice to me."

He sighed. "Right. Sorry. I just—what she must have gone through, this last year..."

"I know. I'm sorry, too. You know I would never abandon her on purpose. But I was the only one who wasn't ready to abandon you; I had to see this through. It took longer than it should have, but I'm bringing both of us back to her, and better versions of us, I think."

I leaned in closer again, resting my head on his shoulder. We were going to be okay.

The old woman came back in not long after; she looked at us for a long, long moment, then smiled. "A few more meals, and one more good night of rest, and then the two of you had best be off, I think. Your reindeer is getting restless, and my neighbor will be needing her cooler back."

We left not long after. I hugged the old woman before we left. I did not think we would have survived without her—not Kai, at least. I would miss her. Kai still seemed a little unsure of himself, but he wasn't one for physical affection with near strangers, anyway. He thanked her sincerely, and we climbed back onto the reindeer's back, the little cooler in my lap; it was full now of lefse, which the woman and I had made together while we let Kai sleep in a little more, still recovering from his illness.

"Good luck, my loves," she said. "I will keep you in my prayers evermore."

The reindeer had been getting restless—we rode on and on as we had before, but even faster, I thought. The reindeer had been unwell, too, from his time with Cecelia; maybe this rest was something we had all needed.

Kai was behind me again, his hands on my waist, a constant reminder that I had succeeded, that despite everything that had gone wrong, I was bringing him home.

At last we reached the ice house, and the ice fisher opened the door just as we approached.

"You've come back! Oh, and with the cooler—sometimes it's decades before I get it back."

We went into the ice house, me and Kai and the reindeer, and the ice fisher unloaded the lefse into a different container.

"Well, tell me what happened. I'm sure you've been through it all already at the chimney house, but you know she's not a fairy; if you have any lingering questions about what you've been through, I'm the one to ask."

I turned to Kai; I still didn't know the details of what had happened before I'd caught up with him. He nodded.

"I was—snowboarding. There were a few of us out there, but it was getting darker, and everyone was heading home; I was the last one left. I was about to leave, and I turned around, and there was a woman there. She looked like a moving ice sculpture, and she—Gerda, I told you how everything seemed ugly and dull, but

147

not—I always loved snowflakes. They never stopped being beautiful. This woman was like a snowflake.

"She grabbed my hands, and she said, 'You don't belong here. Little ice boy—you're too cold for this world. Come with me, and it will be better.'

"And it seemed—it seemed like the thing to do. So I went. She loaded me into a glass-clear sleigh, and we rode through an eternity of blizzards, but I never felt cold. We came to a palace of ice, and she gave me snow cones to eat and ice puzzles to solve, and then she left, and a long, long time went by. Then Gerda came."

I really needed to fill him in on the whole names in fairy land situation.

The ice fisher fairy only nodded, and I picked up the story from when I'd arrived. She stopped me when I reached the part where two pieces of glass appeared to complete the ice puzzle.

"You found these after he'd been crying?"

"Yes."

She turned to Kai. "And after you cried, the whole world looked better and clearer, and you realized for the first time how cold the ice palace really was."

"Um, yeah. Exactly."

She sighed. "I am going to tell you a story older than fairy land itself, and I believe it will explain your whole life to you." One of the many fishing poles she had sitting in buckets, the lines going down to holes below, jerked suddenly to the side. "Just as soon as I've caught this fish."

It was several minutes before she turned her attention back to us. Finally, she set the fishing aside again and said, "This is not the sort of story I usually tell, but I will tell it to you now as my mother told it to me, when I was but a sprite small enough to sleep in thimble. My mother was half human herself, and lived not nearly as long as she ought to have, but when she was born, in human lands far north of yours, the world was young, and all of its components closer together. I don't know much about gods and devils, I'm afraid, so you must decide for yourself how much meaning to give it."

She cleared her throat, and began in a far-off voice, deeper than her usual speaking voice, and more heavily accented. "Long, long ago, in the days when dreams walked the earth, the devil and all his demons gathered together to make what you, in your modern world, might call a funhouse mirror. But it was not for the sort of fun and games one finds at a carnival; it distorted all things it reflected to appear wicked and ugly. The devil caused much mischief and chaos with this mirror, but that was not enough for him. He decided to carry it up to the heavens, so that whenever men tried to look to God, instead they would see only their own wickedness amplified.

"But God would not stand for this, so he granted the devils clumsy hands. The mirror slipped and fell, and shattered into a thousand-thousand pieces, which have been causing trouble ever since. Sometimes a larger piece will be made into a new, smaller mirror, or into a window pane, and of course you can imagine what must come of that. But worse, some very small shards will fly into men's eyes, and distort their vision so that everything in their sight becomes ugly and wicked. And worst of all, some pieces will fly into men's hearts, and those hearts will be hardened to all good things in this world, frozen like blocks of ice."

She looked over at us, as if coming back from a great distance away, and said in her usual voice, "You, young man, I would guess got one in the heart and one in the eye. I've seldom heard tell of one losing those shards of glass, so count yourself lucky—the remains of that mirror are a far worse fate than anything the snow queen could have done to you."

We did not discuss it further. Kai looked shaken; I felt shaken. If the ice fisher was right, magic had first come for Kai years before the snow queen did, and afflicted him—and everyone who cared for him—with a mundane sort of misery he likely never would have escaped without meeting her.

Is that what she meant, about ice in his heart that she hadn't put there? Had she thought he belonged in her ice palace at the top of the world because his heart was frozen solid by some ancient, evil carnival trick?

When your best friend grows up mean, you never suspect it's because of magic. Lesson learned, I guess—expect the unexpected, or something.

The ice fisher fried her latest catches for us, and we ate walleye with lefse and a bit of butter. There was fresh hay for the reindeer this time, too—"I hoped you'd be back again," the fisherwoman said, "and thought I should be prepared to be a good host."

The reindeer occupied himself with the fresh hay happily—he may not need food, here in the winter, but he certainly enjoyed it—and largely ignored us until it was time to leave again. We did not sleep in the ice house, as we had not last time. Kai was still a little shaky and too pale, not fully healed from his illness. But we needed to move on, to get home. Days and nights passed far too quickly here, and our families thought us long dead.

We said our goodbyes, and went back out into the snow. It was thick and heavy on the ground, but it wasn't menacing, as it had seemed when I faced it without Kai, anymore. I took a few steps, sinking into it nearly up to my knees. More snow was still coming down, slow and soft, and some of it not coming down at all, but drifting across the sky—more snow bees, maybe. I didn't want to try to catch one again. Kai was just behind me; he caught up, and caught my mittened hand in his.

"I still like winter best," he said. "That wasn't just the frozen heart."

The sun was setting, and except for the ice house, there was nothing but pale pink sky and snowy ground for as far as we could see in any direction.

"We should build a snow fort again next winter," I said, and he nodded.

"We'll be—next winter will be so weird. Everything will be so weird."

"Because you're unenchanted?"

"No. Well, yeah. But if we've been gone for a year, and we're nowhere near home yet—we're missing our senior year, right now.

Will our whole class be in college without us by the time we get back? Will we have to retake a year and a half of school with the kids who were freshmen when we left? What are we going to tell everyone about where we've been? What am I going to tell college admissions about the huge gap in my high school education?"

I squeezed his hand, and tilted my head up to feel the snowfall on my face. "You worry too much, Kai."

"Well, I have eight or nine years of not really caring about anything to make up for."

"You didn't really—I mean, you cared about things. Some things. Right?"

He shrugged. "Kind of, but everything just felt sort of—far away? It felt like caring what happened next in a book, not about—not about my own life, my own family. I just—everything is so much."

I sat down abruptly on the ground, sinking deep into the snow, pulling Kai down with me. He laughed a little.

"What are we doing?"

"We're sitting down and relaxing. Just feel the snow fall and don't worry for a while. The reindeer will come get us before we get too cold."

I'd pulled him all off balance; he righted himself and scooted closer, and we sat pressed close together in the snow like we had as kids, watching the sky fade too quickly from pink to deepest blue.

When it was properly dark again, we climbed back on the reindeer's back, and on and on and on we rode, until the weather warmed and the snow began to melt, until there were only traces of frost on the ground. At last I slipped off my cloak, and Kai, behind me, slipped off his coat, and after that it was only a few more minutes—by the passage of the sun as well as by my internal clock—before the reindeer slowed to a halt.

I nudged Kai; he took the hint and dismounted. I followed suit, and circled around to face the reindeer.

"I daren't leave the winter lands again. I'm sorry—I'm not a brave beast."

I cupped his head in my hands and pressed a kiss to his velvet-soft snout. "I think you are a very brave beast. Thank you, and I wish you a better life."

He nodded, then turned and ran away, and I stood and watched until he disappeared into the distance.

Chapter 13

When the reindeer was gone I turned back to Kai.

"Okay. We're on our own. The goal is to move south until we reach the newspaper princess, and then she'll help us figure out what to do next."

"The newspaper princess?" he asked.

"Yeah, I have a lot of stories to tell you. The hardest part will be getting through the city—I don't have a map, and I don't trust either of us to navigate around the city without it, and still wind up where we need to be. But we'll have to be careful. The city is where I got grabbed last time."

I was terrified to go back to the city. But everything I wanted was on the other side.

"We're on foot from here?" Kai asked, and I nodded. "Any idea how long a walk it'll be?"

"I was on the reindeer from the city to here, before, and on a sleigh before that. So longer than I took, I guess? But I'm not sure how long that was, really. It's been—time moves strangely here."

"Okay. So we'll figure it out. Let's start walking, and you can tell me about this newspaper princess and your various kidnappings while we go."

The storytelling, on and off between other things, took several days. We were walking along a river, so we were fine for water, but all we had to eat was the dried, salted fish that the ice fisher had crammed into every spare place in our backpacks.

(I have grown to hate dried fish.)

We slept whenever the sun set, taking turns, a few hours each. Without the sleigh to keep me steadily moving past all troubles, I didn't trust fairy land with my eyes closed.

It was many days before I took the time, in the light of day, for a good long look at Kai's face. We had not been face-to-face in full light, without snow blowing between us, since leaving the palace of ice.

"Kai...your eyes."

"What about them?"

They were still the warm brown I'd known all my life, except for the outside edge of each iris, where there was a very narrow line of deep, cold blue.

"Nothing to worry about," I told him. "I think the snow queen just left her mark, that's all."

"What does that mean?"

"They've just got a little blue around the edges. Seriously, don't worry about it."

He stared at me for a long moment, then shrugged and continued walking. I started to tell him about riding through troll country, mainly to have something to say. I wasn't quite sure how to talk to him, without danger and disaster between us. I'd never been shy or uncertain with Kai, before.

"I tried, I tried to pray, in the palace," he said suddenly one day, "but I couldn't remember how."

I'd just prayed over lunch, as I always did; I suppose that's why he brought it up. "What's there to remember? 'Dear God, please help'?"

Kai shrugged.

"What's the square root of eight hundred and twelve?"

"Twenty eight point five," he said immediately.

"You can remember that, but not 'God, help me'?"

"I was enchanted!"

Okay, well, that was true. I couldn't remember praying at all, or even thinking about God, during the time I was enchanted in the cottage. "Sorry," I said.

He shrugged.

"We could pray together," I offered. I'm not really a pray-out-loud kind of girl; my faith is quiet and awkward and private, just like the rest of me. But after all the other things I'd done for Kai lately, one little out-loud prayer shouldn't be too bad.

I'd spent a lot of time praying, on my way to the ice palace, when I had no one but God to talk to. In the sleigh, in Cecelia's bathroom, in her bottom bunk. It was nice to have someone here again who would talk back.

Kai shrugged again. I felt awkward, about the praying, so I shrugged back. "You can pray, at supper," I suggested. "For practice."

"Okay."

~

157

Kai's missing glasses were a problem. I don't know how bad his eyes were, then, but pretty bad. His glasses were really thick.

It was a major safety issue. He couldn't see things like roots or rocks on the ground, to avoid tripping over them. There was a lot of squinting and stumbling around. We had to slow down a lot, and after a while I realized things were easier if we held hands. It wasn't as awkward as I expected it to be.

"I hate this," he said.

"What happened to your glasses, anyway?"

He shrugged. "They must have fallen off somewhere."

"Do you think it was that magic glass that damaged your eyes in the first place? It was about that time."

"Maybe. But I think my mom has glasses too. And I know my grandpa did."

Kai's grandpa died when his dad was a teenager. But there are a lot of pictures around the house. I don't think he's seen his mom since he was old enough to remember it.

Sometimes I worry my parents didn't really want me. I know they didn't...plan for me. But at least they're there. And my bio parents just died—Kai's both abandoned him.

"I didn't plan very well. Next time I have to chase you into fairy land, I'll remember to bring along your spare glasses. And more than seven granola bars."

"I am not getting dragged into fairy land a second time. And if I do, I'm keeping better track of my glasses."

~

Kai was better than me sometimes at filling our awkward silences. He had a lot to think about, I guess, after coming unenchanted. I think sometimes he was thinking out loud, more than he was talking to me. Even if I was the thing he was thinking about.

"I think you stopped feeling like a real person to me," he said one day. "It's not—I mean, everyone did. Nothing outside of me seemed quite real, and none of it made sense. It was like I was seeing everything, and feeling everything, through frosted glass. I was the only thing I could feel properly, so I was the only thing that felt real to me.

"I just—I wanted that glass to shatter. Sometimes. Sometimes I didn't really care; sometimes it was really hard to care about anything. Most times. But sometimes I wanted the glass to shatter, and it seemed like—it seemed like the more upset someone was, the more real they felt.

"So sometimes I was a jerk because I just didn't care. And sometimes I was a jerk because I was trying to goad you into making me...feel things, I guess. And I know both those things suck. And I—it never occurred to me, until you found me in the ice palace, that I could just say 'hey, I think there's something wrong with me; I feel like I'm experiencing the whole world through the shower door.'"

"Maybe you couldn't. Maybe that's how being enchanted works."

"I don't get why you're so determined to act like everything is fine between us just because I got something caught in my eye one day."

"Because you're my friend. I just want you to be my friend again. I just want you back. And if you having something stuck in your eye means I can have that, I'd rather just be happy about it, and let all the drama go. I love you, Kai, but I'm forgiving you for my sake, not yours, okay? So just stop worrying and let us have this."

"Okay," he said. "I can do that. But I am sorry."

"I know you are. But I'd forgive you either way. Oh, look! Raspberries."

He followed me to the little patch I'd spotted. "Are those even in season?"

I shrugged. "Fairy land does what it wants. If it presents me with edible food, I'm going to eat it, and not ask questions."

"Isn't that traditionally how you get trapped in places like this for a hundred years? Or six months out of every year, or something?"

"I've been fed by a few trustworthy people now, and they haven't seemed to think it would affect our chances of getting home."

"Okay, but how trustworthy are any fairies, really?"

I sighed. I was sitting cross legged on the ground by then, gathering raspberries in my skirt, and he was crouched a ways away, not helping. "Kai, you haven't trusted a soul since you were nine years old. Not me, not Grandma, not God. You haven't put faith in anything but numbers and an ice woman in the better part of ten years, and where has it got you?"

"Feverish, half-frozen, and trapped in a palace of ice," he admitted.

"Exactly. You don't have to have faith in fairies. But have faith in me, okay? Have faith in my faith. I'm going to get us home. And we can't get home if we starve to death first. I promise a handful of raspberries isn't going to ruin anything."

"Okay," Kai said. "Okay. You know, the serpent told Eve—"

"Are you seriously citing the Bible to me, Mr. I-tried-to-pray-but-all-I-could-remember-was-long-division? You don't have to eat anything you don't want to. But I'm sick of dried fish, and I have a lapful of raspberries. I'm sure I can eat all of them, if you're not in the mood to help."

Kai settled a little more comfortably on the ground, plucking one of the berries from my skirt and popping it into his mouth. "I do trust you, Gerda. It's just...hard, for me."

"I know. It's hard for me too sometimes. And I guess it doesn't help that the first person you put your faith in after all this time locked you up in an ice palace. Although I think she had good intentions."

"You think everyone has good intentions."

"Yeah, well, just be grateful I do—it got us this far."

Kai shrugged. "This is much better than the fish."

~

We played a lot of do-you-remember, on that walk from the winter lands to the city. That and what I thought of as road trip

161

games—not that I'd been on many road trips. The one where you go through listing animals for every letter of the alphabet, and the one where you have to pack an imaginary suitcase and remember everything in it. Memory games and singing games and the kind that go with hand clapping or jump roping on the playground. Nothing like I Spy, or anything visual, of course.

"Do you remember when we went to the Wisconsin Dells?" I asked. I'd been thinking of road trip games; it was one of the few road trips—one of the few vacations—either of us had ever been on. My parents are too busy, and Grandma doesn't have the money; they've been living on her husband's pension, or something, for as long as I can remember.

There was a special conference for my dad's job down at the Dells, on a long weekend once every five years. The two times I remember going, when I was eight and when I was thirteen, Mom and Dad had me bring a friend, so I would have something to do while they were busy. When I was thirteen I brought Manda, but when I was eight I brought Kai.

"I remember," he said.

"Do you remember the night when it snowed, and we went and sat in the outdoor hot tub?"

"There were like six strange adults there, and they were all drinking."

"They were?"

"They were completely plastered."

"I didn't notice."

"You wouldn't," he said, and it sounded fond. I could imagine him saying the same thing in a completely different tone, a year and a half ago.

"They smelled like my dad," he added.

I don't really know anyone who drinks. Grandma and my parents don't, or anyone at church. I think Manda's parents might, but not when I'm around, and I've never been around them much, anyway.

"A hot tub would be really nice right now," I said. "Even if it was full of drunk strangers."

We hadn't had a proper bath or shower in ages—the water in the stream we were following was much too cold. It would be so good to spend some time in warm, clean water.

"We'll go to the community center," Kai suggested. "As soon as we get home."

"That'll be nice."

We walked in silence for a couple minutes, then Kai said, suddenly, "I'm worried. About Grandma. It's been so long since— she just keeps losing people. And now, both of us, it's—it's too much. It's not fair."

"My parents will look out for her. And everyone else at church." I wanted to say we'd be home soon, but it wasn't true—there was the forest of time ahead, and we were on foot now.

"Your parents, too. You're the only family they have."

I shrugged. "Yeah, well. It's not like they wanted me—probably nice to have a break."

Kai frowned. "Take it from someone whose parents don't—yours love you, Gerda. A lot."

~

"Do you remember Gracie Gregson's tenth birthday party?" Kai asked.

"At the bowling alley?"

He nodded.

"Is that the one where Craig threw up?"

"I think so."

"That was fun. I forgot we used to kind of be friends with Gracie."

"Right. It must have been later that year that she called you a—"

"Yeah," I said quickly. I didn't need to hear it again, especially not in Kai's voice. "At least you've never been a racist jerk." No one was, really, except for Gracie—or Gracie's parents, I guess. A ten-year-old didn't come up with that on her own. Neither of us was allowed to play with her after that.

"Sorry," Kai said. "I didn't mean to bring that up. I was just thinking about pizza."

"Bowling alley pizza?"

"Yeah," he said, wistfully.

"The crust is cardboard and the cheese is plastic."

"So there's a nostalgia factor. It would be better than more dried fish."

"By the time we get home we'll have earned much higher quality pizza than that."

164

We talked a lot about when we got home. I don't think Kai really understood how long a journey it was going to be—he'd been enchanted the first time around. I was just trying not to think about it. We could save months by avoiding any further hostage situations, but making the whole trip on foot would cost us. And the Forest, especially—that could easily take six months or more.

~

On a cool spring night, when the cluster of buildings that made up the city was in sight, maybe a day's walk away, maybe two, we stopped for the night at the base of a wide, rough-barked tree with buds just unfurling into leaves. We sat, the thick roots of the tree wrapping around us; I sank down into the mossy ground, while Kai pressed his back against the trunk. It was my turn to sleep first.

After a minute, he slipped down so he was laying on the ground beside me. "Don't worry," he said. "I won't fall asleep."

We looked up at the sky, most of it visible through the gaps in the still budding canopy of the tree. The stars were very bright; I wondered how they looked to Kai, without his glasses.

(Maybe I shouldn't have been letting him keep watch—he wouldn't see anyone coming until they were practically on top of us, especially in the dark. But I had to sleep sometime.)

"I love you too," he said quietly, and it took me a moment to realize that he was answering what I'd said weeks ago, in the snow queen's palace. I reached out to find his hand in the dark, and we laid there for a while, hand in hand, staring up at the stars.

"The woman in the chimney house called you the brother of my heart," I told him.

"I like it," he said after a moment, which meant that we loved each other in the same way. I fell asleep with my hand in Kai's and woke to the sun shining in my eyes; he'd never woken me for my shift.

Chapter 14

I was terrified to enter the city again. It had been awful last time, even before Cecelia and the robbers. At least I had nothing worth stealing, anymore, and I was pretty sure I was no longer a child by the laws of my own land.

As soon as I got to the newspaper princess, I would know the date again. Just that much longer, that much farther.

The movement of the clock hands as I rode the reindeer—it could be any length of time, and I wouldn't know. Kai didn't look noticeably older, and he hadn't said that I did, either; that was the only real indication I had that it hadn't been years and years since we left home. And really, the way fairies aged—if we aged the way they aged while we were in their world—it could have been years, and we'd never know it to look at each other. The woman in the chimney was human, or had been; she'd looked old, but not nearly as old as she claimed to be.

I just didn't know. I had to set the worry aside until we reached the princess. But I was fairly certain we'd both turned eighteen by now.

We encountered two fairies almost as soon as we stepped through the open gate; they approached us, then stopped suddenly.

"Ice-touched," one whispered to the other, and they shied away from us.

We walked down the street with no trouble. All the fairies gave us the same wide berth, and many of them whispered "Ice-touched." It was...unsettling, but it felt safer than last time I'd been through here. I stuck close to Kai, though he needed me less than he had, walking straight on a clear street. I'd nearly let my guard down by the time anyone tried to interact with us.

"Oh, you found him," said a voice behind me, and I spun around to see Cecelia, standing in the alley. I reached out for Kai's hand, though I knew we'd parted on decent terms.

"I did," I told her.

"Good."

"Is your family around?" I thought I could manage Cecelia, but I didn't want another encounter with the fairies.

"They're on a job. I'm not invited. Why isn't anyone trying to grab you this time?"

"They say we're ice-touched," Kai offered.

"Oooh, really?"

Cecelia leaned forward, much too close, and I took a step back automatically. She pouted.

"Don't be a wuss; I just want to see your eyes."

She came forward again, and I let her this time.

"It's your friend that's ice touched. He really was with the snow queen, wasn't he? I thought you made it up."

"I was," Kai says.

"No one will bother you, then; they're all terrified of the snow queen. They won't serve you, either, though—I'll get you some food if you'll stay a bit and eat it with me."

We could do with food, so it seemed we were stuck with her.

"This is Cecelia," I told Kai. "Don't tell her your name yet—that's a thing here."

Yet. I shouldn't have said yet—that implied that I expected her to be around long enough for Kai to get to know her.

She led us to a little restaurant, and told us to wait while she went inside.

"We need to get food before we leave," Kai said. "Food we can travel with, not just a meal. That fish—I cannot handle another meal of that fish, and we're almost out, anyway. I know she was awful to you, but if she can help us get enough food to get through the next leg of this journey..."

"Yeah. Yeah, I know."

"Was she as bad as me?"

"You were a jerk, Kai. She held me hostage."

"So that's a yes."

"She was infinitely worse, and doesn't even have the excuse of being under a spell. But she is a human child raised by abusive, neglectful fairies that might have kidnapped her, too—I don't think changelings are usually a consensual arrangement—so maybe I can—she meant well, I know that. She just wanted friends. But she didn't know what friendship looked like."

"You don't have to forgive everyone for everything, Gerda. You're allowed to stay mad at people who treat you like crap."

"Yeah, but I'm allowed to forgive them, too. It's my choice."

"And you choose kindness."

"I guess I do."

"I'm glad," Kai said. "I just don't want to hurt you again because you're kinder than I deserve, and I don't want this girl to, either."

Cecelia came back with the food.

"Do you think you could help us get more?" I asked her. "Enough to travel with?"

Her eyes lit up. "That's a thing friends do, isn't it?"

I didn't want to—to use her. But she'd used me for months, so maybe it was fair? "It is," I told her.

"I can get stuff from the house! You can come with me, or you can wait outside, if that feels safer. But I won't let the house keep you this time—it usually listens to me."

We followed her there. Two fairies—men, one who looked human, one with green skin—were approaching the house just as we were, and Cecelia ducked quickly behind a bush to avoid them. We followed her.

"I'm not supposed to be out," she whispered. "We have to wait until they leave."

They stood in front of the house for several minutes, talking. We were only a few feet away, and I was sure that at any moment they'd turn and see us. There seemed to be an ever-shifting collection of fairies in the house, when I'd been there—more than I could keep track of to start with, then more appearing suddenly and acting as if they'd been there all along. I wasn't sure I remembered these two, particularly. But a few that I'd seen had cat eyes, and presumably the accompanying night vision.

At last they went inside, then came out again quickly, carrying large bags. I decided I didn't much want to know what was in them.

We followed Cecelia into the house as soon as they were gone—I hadn't been sure about going inside, but it seemed better than waiting to be spotted in the front yard, if anyone else came back. She took us to her room, by a path I didn't remember taking before. It would have been fascinating how the house moved around, if I'd ever had the room to feel anything but terrified while I was there.

"Stay here," Cecelia said. "It's safest. I'll find food and come back."

I glanced around the room—it was different, though it took me a moment to work out why. "Where are your guinea pigs?"

"Oh, I set them free. Just like you and the reindeer."

Kai opened his mouth; I caught his eyes and shook my head sharply, and he closed it again without saying anything.

Those guinea pigs were probably dead, and Cecelia was old enough to know better. I didn't ask if she'd set the cats and any surviving ants free as well—they at least had a chance of survival, if she had. But Cecelia was fairy-raised, so maybe she really didn't know better. Anyway, there was no helping the guinea pigs now, and we couldn't afford to upset her in the middle of an escape.

"Be right back," she said, and disappeared into the hallway. I sat down on the bottom bunk, and after a moment Kai joined me.

"So you lived here."

"Yeah. It smelled worse, then."

We sat in silence for a few minutes. I didn't want to talk about it—at all, really, but especially with Cecelia somewhere nearby and doing us a favor, in a house that, for all I knew, might literally have ears.

"What are we gonna tell people about your eyes?" I asked. I'd almost thought, before, that the change was just my imagination.

He shrugged. "That is way down on the list of explanations to plan."

"Fair."

Cecelia came back after about a quarter hour, both arms full with dozens of plastic grocery bags. "Some of this'll fit in the backpacks you have. And I have a couple more in my closet. Mine are enchanted, so we can squish stuff down more. Yours look a little enchanted, too."

"They probably are," Kai said.

"Come back with us," I said. It was a sudden impulse, one I regretted almost as soon as I opened my mouth.

"My mother loves me," she said.

"Maybe she does, in her way. But you deserve better." I didn't even know which one of those fairies she considered a mother—

certainly, none had exhibited any maternal behavior while I was watching.

"I can't go back to the human world. I don't belong there."

"There's a whole lot of fairy land outside this house. I know a newspaper princess who might help you find a better part of it. Or if you change your mind, about the human world, she could help you find any family you left behind there."

Cecelia frowned. "Are you—are you sure?"

I glanced over at Kai. He shrugged. "Your call."

"Yeah. I'm sure. It's just—it won't be an easy trip. I wish I still had the sleigh."

"I have to pack!"

"Could we get the sleigh back?" Kai asked, while he and I loaded food into the enchanted backpacks, and Cecelia rushed around her room gathering the things she wanted to keep.

"Cecelia?"

She paused in her frantic packing. "It's kept in the stable down the street; we've crammed a lot of things into our house, but we just couldn't make room for it. It's useless, anyway—no one can get it to drive itself like you did, and beasts don't want to pull it. Can't sell it, can't even strip it for parts. But Mother's too proud to give up on it, so she pays to keep it at the public stables. We need to present a token to get it back—I know where that's kept. But the stablemaster recognizes all our band, and won't give it to a stranger, token or not."

"Won't he give it to you?"

Cecelia shook her head. "I'm just a changeling."

"We can try to steal it back?" I suggested.

Kai frowned. "The two men who were here when we came in—would they be allowed to take the sleigh?"

"If they had the token, but they've left now, and they would never help us steal from Mother, anyway."

"Take us to the bedroom of the one who didn't have green skin," Kai said.

Cecelia turned to look at me; I didn't argue, so she shrugged and led the way down another winding hallway. I fell into step with Kai behind her. "Are you going to—"

"About time I did something useful, isn't it?"

"You've been enchanted. And ill."

"He looked about my height and I know I can do the voice. We'll see what he's got in his closet—pray for big hats. How about the skin tone? I couldn't really make that out, beyond that it was better than the green."

"Near enough to yours, I think. We'll wait until dark to go, and hope this guy isn't friends with the stablemaster or anything."

"Not that I mind stealing his stuff," Cecelia said as she pulled things out of the drawers and tossed them to the ground, "but stealing is my thing, and I thought you guys were in a hurry."

"We're going to get Gerda's sleigh back," Kai said.

"Go find that token," I told her. "Do you have everything else you want?"

She nodded. "Are you—are you sure? About leaving? About me coming?"

"Positive," I said, even though I really wasn't. It was the right thing to do, getting a kid out of this situation, to somewhere she could have a clean room and adults who didn't hit her for introducing herself to people. "The token?"

"On it."

I helped Kai get ready. "Are you sure about the voice? What about the walk?"

"I got enough," he said, and his voice sounded just like the fairy's. "I can do this."

"I got the—" Cecelia stopped abruptly in the doorway. "Oh," she said after a moment. "It's your friend. Right?"

"Right," I told her. "Let's go—we have a sleigh to rescue."

It had been months—probably a year or more now—since I'd thought a drama club was just what Kai needed to stay out of trouble. He really was a great actor, and great at mimicking people, specifically. Usually he used that to make fun of them. But he'd mimicked teachers' voices to get out of trouble before. I was pretty sure he could pull it off on a slightly larger scale.

The stable wasn't far from the house. The three of us went to the stablemaster together, Kai claiming they'd brought me to operate the sleigh for them. It obeyed me, as it always had, and we were through the gates within a half hour.

"It'll carry us through the night," I told the others. "We can sleep. Unless the fairies will come after us?"

"No," Cecelia said. "They won't do anything if it's hard. I'm not worth searching for, and neither is the sleigh. They'll punish me if I turn back up at home, but otherwise they won't bother."

"Not even your mother?" Kai asked.

She bit her lip. "I don't—I—"

"Never mind," I said. "Kai's a jerk sometimes—you can ignore him."

"I thought we weren't telling her my name?"

"I think she's earned it—don't you?"

"Yeah, she has."

"Okay. Bedtime. It's more comfortable than it looks."

We were off. Through the first big barrier, and really, really on our way home.

Chapter 15

It was a very different journey, with two companions in the sleigh. The time between the city and the forest passed quickly, with conversations to have and road trip games to play and all the odds and ends Cecelia had packed.

I'd been nervous to have Cecelia along, but it was good. It made things less boring. We were never going to be close friends, and she frequently got on my nerves, but having other people to be responsible for helped me feel steadier, less anxious. And Kai didn't need to be taken care of so much, now that we were in the sleigh; his blindness didn't matter so much, for the moment.

She was difficult sometimes, though.

"I'm bored," Cecelia whined, now, as she often did at night. "I don't want to sleep yet."

"Well, there's not much else to do in the dark."

"I'm bored," she said again.

"Maybe if you ask nicely, Gerda will tell you a story," Kai suggested. "She's good at that."

Cecelia turned to me. "Please, Gerda?"

"All right." It was a good night, I thought, for a fairy tale. My favorite of the stories Grandma used to tell us had been of the man who swapped roles with his wife for the day, and quickly became overwhelmed. But Kai's favorite had been "East of the Sun and West of the Moon," and she had told it to us so often that I knew the beginning, at least, by heart.

"Once on a time there was a poor woodcutter who had so many children he had not enough food or clothing to give them. Pretty children they all were, but the prettiest was his youngest daughter, who was so lovely there was no end to her loveliness."

I faltered early, at the point when the girl first agreed to go away with the bear, and climbed onto his back. I knew the story, the shape of it, at least, if I could not tell the whole thing word-for-word the way Grandma read it from her book. But it made me think of Grandma, and of everyone and everything else I had been missing for so long, and I—I couldn't. I wanted to cry.

Kai wrapped an arm around my shoulders and continued calmly, "So, when they had gone a bit of the way, the white bear asked, 'Are you afraid?'

"'No,' said the lassie, 'I am not afraid.'"

Kai did know the whole story word for word, because Kai never forgot anything. I listened to it in his steady voice, my head on his shoulder, Cecelia quiet beside us, under the slowly darkening sky. And it felt like home.

~

We reached the forest sooner than I expected—one morning I woke up and found the sleigh about to pass through the trees. I called it to a stop, and waited for the others to wake.

"This is the forest of time," I told Kai and Cecilia both, when they did. "We'll be trapped in our memories, most of the time. Each hour in the forest will be a day everywhere else—we'll lose at least a month and a half of our lives to this leg of the journey. So don't get out of the sleigh—we could lose you forever."

Cecelia nodded solemnly.

"Kai?"

He rolled his eyes. "Yes, Gerda, I've got it. Keep my blind butt in the sleigh, or I'll be wandering an enchanted forest for days that'll turn into years."

"It's not the fun kind of trip down memory lane."

"We'll be fine."

I checked the pocket watch—8:36am—and let the sleigh move ahead.

There is a little girl at the top of a staircase—Cecelia. A woman stands at the foot of the stairs, hands on her hips. "Celia, it's nearly midnight! If you step foot outside your bed one more time tonight, I'll let the fairies take you away."

Forest. I was dizzy; Cecelia vomited, and I think some landed on Kai's shoes. He wrinkled his nose, but didn't say anything. I checked the pocket watch, glowing faintly in the dark woods. Nine o'clock, exactly. Not too bad a loss. But we were experiencing each other's memories.

Kai and I are sitting beneath the rosebush in our front yard, but something feels wrong, feels off.

I summoned the awareness, from wherever in the woods I'd left my body, to realize that it was Kai's memory, not mine.

Kai and I are sitting beneath the rosebush in our front yard. There is a sudden, sharp pain in his eye, and he thinks something has flown into it, but the pain sinks deeper in, and then seems to expand across both eyes, and then fades. A second later there's a pain in his chest, and he tries to ignore it, and focus on Gerda and the roses and the bees.

But things look...funny. A little blurry, so maybe something did fly into his eyes, and it's still there? But not just blurry. Dull and distorted and strange, too. Gerda looks wrong, and the roses look wrong, and the bees look wrong.

The bees are friendly and half tame, because Kai and Gerda are often with them in the flowers. It's not hard to reach out and catch one—he has to—he has to find out what's wrong, why it doesn't look the way it's supposed to, but it won't stop moving so he can look.

So he makes it stop. Gerda shouts, and he doesn't know why—he feels so—

I pulled us back into the present, where Kai's hand was warm in mine. He looked pale and ill.

"That was the day, wasn't it? The day you were first...enchanted, or whatever."

"Must have been," he agreed, and his voice was wobbly and awful. I was surprised that Cecelia didn't try to ask what we were talking about, what was going on, but maybe she was just too disoriented still. I checked the time—10:03. If there was a pattern, the next memory would be mine, and I didn't want to think about what kind of random, potentially private moment in my life I would soon be sharing.

I am sitting next to Manda on her bed. We're fourteen, or nearly—she's planning her birthday party. I don't have birthday parties, not with everyone from school, because they don't like me and I'm trying not to like them either. But everyone will be at Manda's party, because everyone likes Manda. And she asked if that was okay, because I'm her best friend and she wants me to have a good time. But I want her to have a good time, so I said everyone should come.

I'm so nervous. It's not really everyone from school, just all the girls, but that's almost worse. If it was everyone Kai would be there, and Kai wouldn't be any nicer than anyone else, but at least he'd be familiar. I've known all these people since kindergarten—Manda only met them a year or two ago—but they still feel like strangers.

"Gerda? Do you think that would work?"

"Yeah," I tell Manda, even though I wasn't listening. "That sounds great."

The forest, briefly, just long enough to check the watch, and then we're pulled into a memory that must be Cecelia's, because it means nothing to me—a dizzying blur of lights and colors that must make sense to someone who's grown up in fairy land, because she looks pale and miserable on the other end of it.

Kai is sitting at his kitchen table, glasses perched crooked on his nose. He's twelve or thirteen, I think—just at the age when I stopped trying to be friends, or maybe a bit after. He looks nervous.

"Your mother was discharged three days ago," Grandma says. "She's staying with her parents now."

The nerves melt right off of him. "So? You called me in here for that?"

"She'd like to meet you."

"Yeah, no. Not happening."

Grandma nods. "Her mother called me this morning to discuss it. I told her you probably wouldn't feel ready for that, but maybe she could write a letter."

"Oh, so my mom's mom does know our phone number. Funny how this is the first time in thirteen years she's used it."

"Your other grandparents—"

"Mom can write me a letter, if she wants. I'm not reading it, but she can write it."

"Kai, your parents—"

"Suck. My parents suck, and I don't want anything to do with either of them, or the other set of grandparents. Can I go now? I have homework."

Grandma sighs. "Yes, Kai, you can go. We'll have dinner at six."

"Kai," I said, because he'd never told me about that, but we were whisked away again before I could say anything else.

A Christmas play. We're tiny children, a memory I remember more from home videos than from the event itself. I'm an angel, Kai's a sheep. The scene shifts—I'm a shepherd, Kai's a Wise Man, bellowing his two-word line ("And myrrh!") with great enthusiasm.

The year I was Mary. The year Kai was Gabriel. The year Kai was too old for that kind of thing, and I was a quiet background character, whispering lines to forgetful little kids. The feeling of itchy little halos, wings made of wire hangers that constantly bent out of shape. Little boys fighting over who got gold, who got frankincense, who got myrrh. A thousand little snapshots of our childhood.

The forest.

A fairy woman kissing scrapes and bruises on a younger Cecelia's knees, the injuries healing in an instant.

Kai again.

"Don't worry, child," the snow queen says, and presses ice cold lips to his forehead. "You were not meant for warmth, but it will be better here; it will be better."

Forest. I checked the time, called it out to the others.

We're at the park chasing fireflies, and I can't tell if it's my memory or Kai's. In this moment, we are in sync, we are one child. The stars are bright and the bugs are brighter, and it's ice cream social night.

The ice cream has long since melted and been packed away, and most people have gone home. My parents have gone home, but Grandma, indulgent, is waiting for us to wear ourselves out. It's summer; there's nowhere to be in the morning, nothing to wake up for.

We wear ourselves out eventually, and lie on our backs in the middle of the playground. Fireflies land on our faces, on our hands, on our toes.

The forest.

A fairy is slapping Cecelia.

The forest again.

Kai is standing in the living room with his father.

"It's your birthday; custody is your call now. You can come home with me, or you can stay here, but if you stay that's it," and he devolves into language I don't care to repeat—he calls Grandma a bad word.

"You mean your mother?" Kai asks. Dad doesn't answer. "Well, that's a tough call, but I think I'm going to have to go with the woman who knows my birthday was actually a month ago."

Back in the forest, Kai was white and shaking. I wrapped an arm around his shoulders before checking the watch again.

"He's not any meaner to me than he is to anyone else," I say.
"That doesn't make it okay."
"I know that. I just meant—it isn't personal."
Manda sighs.
"You can't turn love on and off, Manda. I look at him, and I see the little boy who saved up three months of allowance money to get the doll I wanted for my birthday. I see trick-or-treating in matching costumes, and building snowmen, and digging for treasure in the backyard. I don't trust him, and I don't rely on him, but I—I don't love him for his sake. I love him for mine. And I love him because no one else will. And I love him because if I go out and sit in the snow with him, I can have my eight-year-old life back. Things can be easy. I can forget the bad stuff. And no one else can give me that."
"I would if I could."
"I know, Manda. I love you, too."
I came back to the forest with a desperate longing for my other best friend. She wasn't there; I pressed closer to Kai instead.

The next several hours passed in a fever-dreamy haze. I made sure to call out the time every time we came back to the forest. It didn't matter nearly so much now—I didn't have the deadline I'd had when I was looking for Kai, and the newspaper princess could tell us the current date when we reached her. But I didn't want to grow complacent and stop tracking time, then come out the other end to find years had passed.

It took us fifty-two hours to reach the other end of the forest, and as soon as we were clear of it, and our hours were counted, we paused the sleigh and slept, too stressed and exhausted to think of anything else. I slept with one hand wrapped around my pocket watch, and one hand in Kai's, and the three of us woke all huddled together under a shining sun.

All the dangers were done. We were safe. We had only to make our way to the newspaper princess, and she would tell us how to get home, and all would be well. We were safe, and the trouble was nearly over.

We had got through the forest in about the time I'd expected—a couple hours longer than last time, which added up to a couple days, but a three hour difference is probably within the expected range of variation for that kind of thing.

That forest—I hadn't just seen their memories; I'd felt them. The three of us were tied together by lives of aching loneliness.

But we didn't have to be. Not me and Kai. All those years we spent one wall apart—some stupid bits of broken glass keeping us both alone.

The devil made a funhouse mirror—well, screw him. We won. We won.

Chapter 16

It was properly summer, on the other side of the forest of time. (We'd lost so much time.)

When we were all awake, Cecelia kicked off her shoes and hopped out of the sleigh.

"Don't go far," I told her.

"Just keep the sleigh going—I'll walk with it for a while. It's so nice out! I haven't been somewhere so nice in ages."

She raced ahead sometimes, and wandered off in different directions, but she kept pace with the sleigh well enough that I didn't worry about losing her. And I had a moment alone with Kai, for the first time since we'd picked her up in the city.

"All right?" I asked him.

"Fine."

"Are you—"

"I don't want to talk about it," he snapped.

"Sorry."

"Sorry," he echoed a moment later. "I just—"

"We don't have to talk about it. Do you want to get out of the sleigh?"

"When I can't see two feet in front of me? No thanks."

"Okay. Animal alphabet?"

"Sure, why not?"

It was a gorgeous day, the sun warm on our skin, birds singing in the distance. And we were going home. We were going home. Just a few more days until we reached the mountains, another week or two on the other side until we reached the newspaper palace. Then one more forest, and we were home.

I had a horrible headache the next morning, the kind where it feels like someone is driving knives into the back of your head. There was no reason for it—I was sleeping and eating well enough, and Cecelia was quiet for once, hanging over the edge of the sleigh to stare at the landscape.

"You okay?" Kai asked quietly. If we were quiet enough, maybe we could have a conversation with just the two of us, without Cecelia noticing and inserting herself. (She was growing on me. Still annoying, but not horrible, and sometimes I enjoyed her company. I liked to have time with just Kai, though, when I could. It was Kai that was my friend, Kai that I had crossed fairy land to rescue, and Cecelia was just along for the ride.)

"My head hurts."

"Drink some water, and close your eyes for a little. I'll make sure Cecelia stays quiet."

"Thanks." I took the water he offered, and leaned back on the bench, and thought absently about how different he seemed, in so little time.

He had been sweet, when he was a little boy. I remember that, remember people saying what a sweet little boy he was, remember how careful and gentle he was, herding bugs off the sidewalk so no one would trample them, fishing them out of swimming pools so they wouldn't drown. And then he got mean, sometimes a little at a time and sometimes all at once, his always-honesty becoming cruelty, his fascination with little, vulnerable things centering more around understanding them than protecting them—and understanding them seemed to end, or even start, with them dying.

Since I got him, he'd snapped at me a few times. Lost his temper when he was stressed. But he apologized after. And mostly—mostly he'd been sweet again. He was Kai. He was my Kai again, and that meant that he—that he'd been there all along. That meant that somewhere inside the boy who picked on me for years, there was still the boy who was my best friend, who loved me as much as I loved him.

His love for me, for Grandma, for all the little bugs on the sidewalk, wasn't strong enough to break through the enchantment of the devil's mirror. And that—that did hurt, a little. But it was also a relief, that Kai was never really a stranger to me.

I fell asleep there beneath the bright shining sun, head still pounding, and woke up to the sound of soft voices—Kai and Cecelia, Kai telling her something, her occasionally asking questions. He was good with her, when he could be patient. He'd been becoming more patient, over the weeks since we'd left the snow queen's palace. I'd missed his patience.

I thought this new version of Kai would be more useful at helping with math homework. Which would be good, since we were now way behind the rest of our class.

Oh, going home was going to be such a mess. Making up school, finding an explanation for where we'd been, even explaining Kai's apparent personality transplant. I wanted—badly—to be back home, but it wasn't going to be easy.

Chapter 17

Our first night in the mountains was the first time I'd been truly scared in a long time. It was an ordinary enough evening, the night air warm and the night sky moonless, but bright with stars. The rocky outcroppings we'd seen over the last few days had grown, and the sleigh was moving steadily upwards. Cecelia was nodding off already, and I was tired, too.

"Someone—someone is singing," Kai said.

I sat up. I didn't hear anything. But I had, a few times, the last time I came through the mountains.

Kai moved to stand—I grabbed his arm. "What are you doing?"

"Who's singing?"

I thought of old picture books about men in togas. Sirens, singing. Men, drowning. I thought of the stories I'd heard—mostly from Grandma, but a few, fuzzy and half-recalled, from the witch in the cottage—about Huldra, which I didn't think were exactly the Scandinavian equivalent of sirens, but I wasn't taking chances.

I'd lost Kai to one beautiful, magical woman already. He was straining in my grip, like he was going to hop out of the sleigh and go chasing after singers I couldn't hear, blind and in the dark.

"Do your times tables."

"What?"

"You heard me. One through twelve. Go. Now."

There was a long moment of silence in the dark. "Fine," he huffed, finally, and threw himself back against the seat, wrenching his arm out of my grasp. Grandma used to make him do that, whenever he got particularly worked up about something; he had usually calmed down, and was thinking a little more clearly, by the time he was through.

I waited a few minutes.

"Do you still hear the singing?"

"No."

"Tell me if you do."

He fell asleep not long after, and nothing happened that night. But I stayed awake until the sun rose, terrified that siren trolls would come to take him away from me.

In the morning, he didn't remember. Even more worried, I told Cecelia what had happened.

She frowned. "He's a mortal man, so more vulnerable to that kind of thing than us—than girls. And already once-enchanted— that makes him even more vulnerable. But he's also ice-touched, so once they got him, they wouldn't be able to keep him."

"So there's no real danger?" Kai asked.

"Oh, no. Once they found they couldn't keep you, they'd set you loose to wander the mountains, until you died or lost your mind."

"Oh."

"Just hold his hand all night until we're through this," she told me. "He belongs to you—you claimed him from the snow queen herself. As long as you're holding on to him, no one else can take him."

He heard the singing for the next three nights, and I clung to him and made him do math while Cecelia slept through the danger.

~

It was so good to be in the sleigh again. I could hardly begin to imagine what a nightmare the forest of time would have been without it, and now the mountains—I didn't know how the sleigh was able to go so smoothly through the mountains, but I knew that on foot it would have taken us weeks, at least. Kai was still half blind, and Cecelia utterly unable to stay focused on the task at hand. She was constantly being distracted by whatever we rode by; if we were on foot I was sure she'd have run after whatever caught her eye, and I would be constantly chasing after her. The sleigh kept her in place, and kept us moving steadily no matter what she was doing. Except for when she left the sleigh, but I'd managed to keep her there for the most part, now that we'd left the meadows for a rockier, more winding terrain.

"She is driving me crazy," Kai whispered.

"Just be thankful you've never been trapped in a small space with her and a dozen untrained, unwashed animals."

"Why did we bring her again?"

"Because we're good people, and it was the right thing to do."

"If you say so."

"You know, being mean in whispers is real progress for you."

He rolled his eyes. "I'm not saying anything you're not thinking."

Well. He had me there.

"Look, look!" Cecelia shouted. "Those rocks are moving!"

I looked up. The sun had just set, streams of gold still flowing out behind it. A troll, then, farther north than most I'd seen.

They hadn't seemed much interested in me or the sleigh last time, but I hadn't been shouting at them. I grabbed Cecelia's shoulder to pull her back down onto the bench. "It's just a troll," I said quietly. "You needn't be shouting at it." I wasn't really worried about this kind of troll. Only the ones that might be singing.

"A troll? Really?"

"Quieter. You've never seen one? Haven't you been living in fairy land since you were a little girl?"

"Only in the city. Trolls don't come into the city."

"Someone tell me what's going on?" Kai asked. The troll was too far away for him to make out the motion, even without the darkening sky.

"Remember I told you about the trolls?"

He nodded.

"It's just another, a little farther north than usual. It won't bother us as long as we don't bother it; we just need to sit here quietly."

"I wish I could see," he said.

"I wish I'd brought a camera."

"Oh, I have one of those," Cecelia said, turning to dig through one of the backpacks she'd brought. "You can have it, I guess—there's a bit of film left."

"You're giving me one of your things?" I asked.

She shrugged. "Well, you gave me freedom and an adventure. And friendship. And I'm not any good at picture taking, anyway. All of mine came out blurry, or just pictures of my fingers."

"Thank you, Cecelia." I wrapped an arm around her shoulders for a quick hug, then turned to Kai. "The light's no good for a photo now, especially if we'll only get a few. I'll photograph a troll for you next time I see one, okay? Right as the sun goes down, before it gets really dark, and when we're a little closer to one."

He nodded. "Thanks, Gerd."

I leaned in closer, putting my head on his shoulder. "I know it's hard, without your glasses."

"You crossed fairy land and got kidnapped twice, I can handle a little blindness."

I saw Cecelia wince in my peripheral vision. That was still a sore point, for both of us. "It's not a competition, Kai. Your spare glasses are in the drawer of your nightstand, in your bedroom. You'll probably need a new prescription—it's been a year—but they'll hold you over. As soon as we get home."

As soon as the sun began to dip in the sky the next day, Cecelia and I were on watch for trolls, so I could photograph one for Kai before it got too dark. Of course the trolls didn't move in daylight, but I was hoping to catch one just as the sun went down, before the light drained out of the sky. One that was properly moving, maybe a few interacting with each other, so it didn't look like we'd just found some rocks in interesting shapes. (I was thinking mostly of Kai, with the camera, but also a little of home. I wasn't sure we could ever tell the truth, but if we tried, photographic evidence would be helpful.)

"There!" Cecelia shouted, leaning over the edge of the sleigh. "There, over by that tree. Hurry, Gerda!"

She was loud enough the trolls—a group of three, just waking up for the night, beneath a scraggly, half dead tree—turned to look at us. Parents and a child, I thought—one was much smaller than the others. We were maybe fifteen feet away, close enough to make me nervous, but I leaned over to get a shot as close as possible.

The baby troll made a confused, indignant sound when the flash went off, and the parents crouched down to comfort it, ignoring us. The sleigh moved on.

(Soon the trolls would be gone. The snow queen would come to take them home, and that baby would have a palace to play in. I was glad. It was cute, as cute as something can be when it's as much stone as person.)

Cecelia's camera was a Polaroid. The photo came out, and I shook it to speed up the development, Kai leaning over my shoulder. "Did you get it?"

"I think so. Give it a minute."

The color bloomed onto the paper, and I handed it over; Kai held it close to his face to see better. "Cool."

We passed through the mountains, seeing fewer and fewer trolls as we went—we were going south, and they were moving north now, drawn, perhaps, back to the snow queen. They had so far to go, though. And so did we. The crow, I thought, would be glad at least—he'd said they were too far south.

I was just tired. So tired. It had been over a year now of travelling through another world, all to find Kai, and I did it. I had him. But we had such as long way to go yet, and even when it was done—it was never going to be done.

We would have to explain—or try to explain—where we'd been, why we'd been gone for so long. And there was no way to explain, no way I could tell my Mom and Dad "I followed Kai into fairy land and crossed it over the course of months, facing fairies and assorted kidnappings, to rescue him from the snow queen, in a palace of ice at the top of the world."

They would—I had no idea what they would do, but it wouldn't be fun. There was no potential future where they believed me. Either they would think I was lying, or they would think I'd lost my mind, and I had no idea which of those options was worse.

And Kai—Grandma would be—Kai's parents are a mess. And Kai doesn't lie. Ever. Even when he should, to be polite. The only time he says something that isn't true—or that he thinks isn't true—is when he's being sarcastic. So if we went home and told Grandma that we went to fairy land—she'd definitely think Kai lost his mind. I've never seen his mom—I'm not sure he's ever seen his mom—but I know from overhearing whispered adult conversations as a kid that she's a drug addict who's been in and out of jail and mental institutions.

But if we both had the same insane story, would that lessen the likelihood that we'd lost our minds? Would we lose our minds in the same way, at the same time?

"What's wrong?" Kai asked. Cecelia was asleep; we were as close to alone as we'd get for a long time.

"What are we going to tell everyone?"

He was quiet for a long moment. "I don't know," he said finally.

"I don't want—there's no way they won't worry about us. But I don't want them to—to have to keep worrying, the rest of our lives."

"We'll tell as much of the truth as we can. We weren't together, at first. You fell asleep searching for me and woke up in an unfamiliar place. We—we can—I don't know, Gerda. We disappeared for over a year, and the only places we could feasibly have gone were into the river—which would be instant death—or into the forest, which isn't nearly large enough to justify that kind of absence. We would have died in the cold or we would have wandered back out of it within a couple hours. There's no way to explain this without making ourselves out as either lunatics or jerks who abandoned their loved ones on purpose, unless we lean into the kidnapping angle, which will have everyone panicking and wasting time and resources searching for someone they'll never find."

"What if we made up a description for the kidnapper, and they found someone who matched it, and that person's whole life was just—"

"Yeah," he said. "We can't lie about anything in enough detail that it could potentially lead anyone searching to someone real."

"We abandoned our families and let everyone think we were dead for well over a year. We have no rational explanation. We're missing our senior year of high school. We are going to be in so much trouble."

Kai sighed. "We'll think about it. I'll think about it, but let's be real—this is on you. I'm not the creative one."

"Great. Thanks."

"Go to sleep. We're not going to solve this tonight, and it sounds like we have plenty of time still to think about it."

"A few weeks, at least."

Chapter 18

Cecelia was, for all her flaws, unfailingly cheerful. Kai was always moody, and my anxiety was steadily rising as I got closer to home and to facing the reality of what I'd done, or what it would look like I'd done, from the other end. It was good to have her. She brought us both out of ourselves.

As we left the mountains behind, I was gladder and gladder for her. I missed the trolls, though we'd never exactly interacted with them. I was anxious to see the princess again, and more anxious to be home, but I dreaded it, too. Cecelia kept up a steady stream of chatter, mostly stories about her time with the band of fairy robbers. She was completely devoid of guilt over any thefts or grand cons she recounted, but it didn't bother me so much now that I was far away from them, from any danger they held.

She chattered, and Kai sulked, and I worried, as we moved farther and farther from the mountains.

At last, there was a small white form visible in the distance, which would, in a few days' time, become a palace all made of paper.

"We'll reach the newspaper princess soon," I told the others. Kai, bored and blind and likely half-asleep, roused himself just enough to acknowledge it. Cecelia leaned forward in her seat, to get a better look at the barely-visible shape.

"And—and I'm to stay with her?"

"If you like. Or we can ask her to help find you another place to stay. Or you can continue on to Minnesota with us, and maybe we could find your birth family."

I hoped she didn't choose the last option. It seemed humans who spent considerable time in fairy land didn't age as quickly as we did at home, and I had no idea how long Cecelia had been here. I doubted she'd have any idea herself.

She frowned. "I don't think I'd like to leave fairy land. Do you think—do you think she'll like me?"

"I'm sure she will. Don't you think so, Kai?"

He looked up at us. "Sure."

Well, that was probably the best I could expect, considering Kai had never met the newspaper princess, either.

"Do you think I'll like her?" Cecelia asked next.

"Definitely."

"Okay. I'll stay, if I like her and she likes me. But if we don't like each other I'll have to go somewhere else. Maybe I can join the trolls. Or keep the sleigh and be a wandering brigand. I'd be a very good brigand."

"I'm sure you would."

After a few minutes she resumed her chatter, though there were definite nervous undertones, now. I leaned back against the bench with Kai.

"All right?" I checked.

"Didn't realize someplace like fairy land could be so boring."

"It's only because we're just riding, and you can't see anything—can't feel any different from a long car ride, really."

"Exactly."

"Well, things'll be more interesting once we reach the palace. You can see things all close-up."

"You're not paying attention," Cecelia complained.

"Sorry, Cece. Go on, we'll listen."

~

I watched the sleigh closely as we approached the palace, to see if it would change back to newspaper. I rather hoped it would, but it stayed the same bright red it had been since shortly after we left.

The palace was even more impressive at the second approach than it had been at the first, so long ago—the incredible whimsy of it without the dread I'd felt before, thinking Kai may be a prisoner somewhere inside.

I got a picture of it, a good one, as close up as I could manage and still get the full thing in. Then I used another bit of our precious, limited film to take one of me and Kai and Cecelia, squished together in the sleigh, smiling. Cecelia was a friend, really, after everything, and I wanted a photo to remember her by.

It came out well. Kai had that distant, unseeing look in his eyes that he always had without the glasses, and we were rather filthy, but we all looked happy. We were all happy, just then. I'd succeeded in rescuing Kai, and I'd managed to rescue Cecelia, too.

The sun was bright and the sky impossibly blue, and it was a lovely, lovely day to be in fairy land.

~

The newspaper princess must have seen us coming; she met us at the front door. It was a shame, I thought, that Kai wouldn't be able to make out the text dancing across her forehead.

"You've found him!"

"I have. Guys, this is the newspaper princess I told you about. Princess, this is Kai, and this is Cecelia, who we picked up in the city. We were hoping you might be able to take care of her, or find someone who could."

The newspaper princess clapped her hands. "A changeling child! Oh, how quaint. Of course she may stay, but first she must take a dozen baths."

"They're just as dirty as I am," Cecelia protested.

"True," said the newspaper princess, "but they smell of sweat and reindeer, and you smell of deceit and rodent urine."

I didn't know how deceit smelled—I hadn't noticed any lingering scent of rodent urine, but maybe fairies had stronger noses.

"I hope Kai and I can get at least one bath each, too."

"Certainly. Come in, come in. We can unpack and put the sleigh away later. I'll take you to the bath, then tell my prince you've come back."

~

She escorted us to three separate bathrooms, so we could all shower at once; Cecelia's was connected, the princess said, to the room she would be staying in.

"Take your time to get settled—we'll get to know each other in a bit. Gerda, come find me when you're clean? I'll be in the library."

"Sure."

I tried to collect Kai on my way back downstairs, but he was still showering.

"I have a year and a half of showers to make up for," he said when I knocked on the door. "I'll find you when I feel more like a person and less like a dust bunny."

Really, I think he was just anxious. He was never good at admitting when he was nervous. But he hadn't really been around anyone but me and Cecelia since he first took off with the snow queen, and the newspaper palace was more glaringly magical than most of the things he'd encountered since leaving the ice palace. Or at least, he was able to get a better look at it than most of the other stuff. He was hiding in the shower because showers are normal, and he didn't want to deal.

I let him hide, and went to meet the princess. The library wasn't hard to find, even though I'd never been in it, and the whole palace was made up of reading material. I think maybe it was enchanted like Cecelia's house, so the hallways moved. The princess was waiting for me there; she stood when I walked in.

"Now, Gerda, I have a gift for you, as I promised." She gestured toward a great stack of newspapers.

"Are those..."

"Your family, darling. I've circled the relevant articles with a red pen, so you can find them quite easily. Of course, most of the articles aren't in English, so I've translated them as well." She held up a thick, battered notebook; I had no idea where she'd pulled it from. "I've copied the headings of each section circled, just as they were printed, and the translations are written out beneath. Now, I know you mustn't linger here—you have loved ones waiting for you, or you would had they not already given up hope. You must hurry, to spare them more pain. So you must take all of the newspapers and the notebook home with you, and read them at your leisure there."

"Are you sure you don't mind me taking your papers? These made up the walls and floors of some rooms, didn't they? And I've already—um. De-papered your sleigh." And ripped several papers into rodent bedding.

"Nonsense. There are always more newspapers—thousands every day. And you need these ones far more than I do. Besides, the sleigh was only an enchantment; all of mine come out that way. I suppose it lost its newspaper-y qualities quickly as you left the confines of my realm?"

"It did."

"It was only a thing. I can conjure another, if I want the pattern the next time I take it in my head to travel. Or maybe my new changeling child would rather steal us some transportation."

"How did you know she was a thief?" I'd meant to tell her, of course, before leaving them. But it hadn't come up yet.

"I know everything that goes on in my house, and she's been at the silverware drawers since we left her. It's unfortunate I have no actual silver in my kitchens—she would be welcome to hoard all of my spoons and forks in her room, if it would make her feel better."

"Oh, that's another thing—the hoarding. Look out for that, if she's staying here; her last bedroom was basically a dumpster slash zoo. Not a great place to be."

The princess smiled, and the text danced across her face. "We will make it work, I'm sure. If it's a zoo she wants, there are certainly enough newspapers to build several stables and enclosures. You may have noticed I have a bit of a hoarding problem myself; perhaps I can help her manage the impulse more tidily."

I was sure if anyone could, it would be her.

I would miss her. The princess. Cecelia too.

"If you can fetch your friend from the shower, we'll all have dinner together, then rest. In the morning you must go home, but one good night of sleep first, I think. For I'm afraid you'll have to walk from here. My sleigh will only become less—well, less in my style, as you travel away from my lands, but still into fairy land. But as you travel out of my lands and back toward your own, it will break down entirely. And I'm afraid it might attract unwanted attention from the witch you met before, who otherwise should be quite disinterested in you. She seeks out children who are lonely and vulnerable; you are not lonely anymore, and you are not a child now, either."

"That's fine—we're good walkers. I was wondering, though, if you could help with something else before we leave?"

"Anything," she said. "Well, I'll try, at least. I fancy I can do most things anyone might want."

"Kai wears glasses usually, but he lost them sometime with the snow queen, and he's been practically blind since I got him back. He has spares at home, but that's still a ways away, and it's hard to walk when you can't really see."

The princess wilted, and all the text on her face sunk slowly down, sort of dripping down the chin and onto her neck.

"I'm sorry—glasses are such tricky magic. I always get them wrong. Every year I have to take my prince back home to the eye doctor for new ones."

A pause, then she brightened, and words crept across her cheeks again. "Oh, but he has spares, too. And old ones still sitting around. Perhaps—if you find Kai, and I find the glasses, we will see if they might do. Meet me back here in a few minutes."

Promises of potentially regaining vision got Kai out of the bathroom quickly. He was all pruney, of course, and his hair was dripping onto the paper floors, but he looked happier than I'd seen him in a while. Kai likes being clean. And he likes being in control, too. Not—I mean, he's not controlling. But he likes to be in control of himself, in control of the situation. And that's hard to do when you can't see.

He put on the glasses. He frowned.

"Um. I don't think we have the same kind of bad eyesight."

"No good?" I asked.

He started to shake his head, then stopped abruptly. "They're making me kind of dizzy."

"I'm sorry," the princess said.

Kai shrugged. "It's fine. Thanks for trying."

She nodded. "Go dry your hair, then—you're dripping everywhere, and it's nearly dinnertime."

"Sorry," I said on his behalf, and hurried him back to the bathroom.

"Sorry," I said again, to him, sitting on the countertop as he dried his hair with a fluffy towel apparently made out of the sports section.

"I pretty much knew I wasn't gonna be able to see until we got home. It's not much farther, right?"

"I don't think so? Only I had that little kidnapping and amnesia situation between home and here, so I'm a little fuzzy on the details. And we'll have to walk—apparently the sleigh doesn't work in that direction."

"That's fine. I don't—I'm not sure I'm in that big a hurry to be home, anyway. I mean, I miss Grandma. And my glasses. But—it's gonna be weird. Isn't it?"

"I guess, probably." I took a moment to think about it—really think about it. Tried to imagine going to school and doing homework and helping at church and listening to my parents, after all this time on my own, being in control of my own life and plans and schedule, with the exception of the kidnapping incidents. And being lonely. So lonely, until I got Kai back. "Weird. But it'll be good, too."

We saw Cecelia again at dinner, clean and dressed in new clothes a bit too big, and the prince, who hadn't made an appearance earlier.

He looked much the same as he had when I saw him last, but there were a few words printed across his right cheek. The princess had told me that he would become less like me, and more like her; I suppose that is what she meant. He acted just the same, and seemed happy.

It occurred to me that Kai and I both had been in fairy land for over a year; had we changed in some way?

Well, we were certainly not the same selves we'd left behind. But that was growing up, I think. And dis-enchantment, in Kai's case. But was there something more, some deeper change that I hadn't noticed?

I asked her, when we got a moment alone later in the night. And about Cecelia, too, who seemed mostly like a girl a bit younger than me, but occasionally alien and strange.

"Fairies put down roots. Our environments become a part of us, and we become a part of our environments. And poor little humans who get caught in our orbits tend to—well, get caught. Travellers soak in little bits of fairy land wherever they go, and never take in too much of one thing to overwhelm them."

"What about your husband? Will he become overwhelmed?"

"I don't think so. I am cautious of the risk, and I want badly for him to always be the self I fell in love with. We have discussed the possibility, though. We discuss it often. He will be fine, I think. And

Cecelia will need some help, some guidance, but she'll come out well too, if I do my job correctly. And really, I've always wanted a little girl."

"But me and Kai, we'll—"

"You'll be fine. I think, if anything, you have only become more yourself since I last met you."

"I feel like myself, I think."

She nodded. "I should warn you, though. Your friend. Things are different here, Gerda. He's a good boy, I'm sure, but cruelty is a hard habit to break. You may find, at home, that he falls back into it. He is kind to you because he cares for you. I'm sure he'll be kind to his grandmother, and anyone else he cares deeply about. But for the rest of it—I imagine you will have to remind him to be kind, sometimes. You may need to be his conscience for a while, until he remembers how to do it for himself."

"I can do that," I said, though I hoped I wouldn't have to.

"Good. It's bedtime, I think. You have a journey to resume come morning."

But that was later. Late, late as the moon faded out and the sun peeked over the horizon, sitting at a small table with her, sipping hot chocolate, as the others slept upstairs. A few last moments with the newspaper princess, who'd become my friend, and who I'd likely never see again.

Right after dinner, we ate apple tarts and ice cream, then moved to the next room and crowded all together for a photo on Cecelia's polaroid.

"We won't all fit in the shot," Kai said.

"Oh, we just need a bit of distance." The princess waved her hand, and a tripod made, predictably, of newspaper appeared. "Say cheese," she told us, and the camera flashed.

It printed beautifully, all of us bright and happy and magical, on a newsprint backdrop, and I tucked it carefully away with the other photos.

~

In the morning we ate breakfast, then dressed and packed. I put back on the same clothes I'd been wearing all along, though there were other, newer things available. This dress and these boots had taken me across fairy land and back—I wanted them to take me home, too, to remind me where I'd been.

Kai must have had the same idea; he was even wearing the same mismatched boots he'd picked up in the ice palace, though they were well out of season.

(And maybe the newspaper princess had anticipated our choices, because everything had been magically cleaned overnight.)

Our bags were ready for us, mine now stuffed with all the newspapers, but there was still magic at play, and they didn't take up nearly as much space—or weigh nearly as much—as I thought they should have.

I hugged the newspaper princess, and the prince as well. Cecelia didn't come downstairs to see us off; she'd called out her goodbyes through the closed newspaper door of her new bedroom. Kai hadn't known the newspaper princess and prince long enough for hugging, but we all said our goodbyes with sadness. I knew I would not likely see the newspaper princess again, though I had the papers she'd given me and the photo I'd taken.

I took Kai's hand, and we set off on foot, into the forest.

Chapter 19

"So what's up with the huge stack of newspapers?" Kai asked when we stopped to eat some of the food the princess had packed for us.

"The newspaper princess collected them for me, after the first time I met her. They're about my family—my bio dad's family, in Taiwan. She even translated the articles for me."

"That's cool. Does it—does it bother you, not knowing about them?"

"A little. I don't—I don't miss my parents. My first parents. I have a family, and they're not—they're not perfect, but I wouldn't want to trade them for anyone else. It just—Mom and Dad don't know anything about my bio dad. I could have aunts and uncles and grandparents and cousins in Taiwan still, who maybe never even got told that my dad died, or what happened to me. And I— it's not super easy, being the only Asian person in our entire town. I've never even met anyone who looked like me when I was old enough to remember, and that—that does suck."

Kai nodded. We packed up our things and continued on our way, and a few minutes passed before he spoke again.

"You saw—in the forest of time—you saw my mom wanted to meet me, when I was thirteen."

"Yeah."

"She did write a letter. I never opened it. She went to jail again six months later, then rehab, and I don't know where she ended up after that. She never tried to contact me again, anyway, and Grandma just got information about her secondhand sometimes—my grandparents on that side never had any interest in me, except for when my mom tried to reach out, they cared enough to look up Grandma's phone number then, I guess. But I—I still have that letter, unopened, in my dresser at home."

"Do you want to meet her, now?"

"No. I—I really don't. I wish I never met Dad. I thought—when I was thinking about it, when we got through the forest—I thought maybe it was the glass, that made me just not care, not want them to be in my life. But I've been thinking about it, and I still don't care about them, still don't want anything to do with them. And I don't—is that bad?"

"I don't think so. I don't think you have to welcome back the people who hurt you."

"You would."

"And I've been told that's unhealthy."

He laughed, barely. "I just—if any of my family outside of Grandma cares even—even a little bit, then us turning up alive— I'm afraid I'm going to have to deal with them, and I don't want to. And I'm afraid I won't have to deal with them, because they don't even care if I'm dead or alive, and I don't—I don't care, but I still want them to. It's stupid."

"It's not. It's not stupid, wanting to be loved. Wanting the people who should love you to be the kind of people you could love."

"It feels stupid," he said.

"It's not. It's kind of how I felt about you for a bunch of years— are you calling me stupid?"

"Of course not."

"Good."

We walked in silence for a few minutes.

"You're allowed to want your parents to love you, Kai. And you're allowed to love someone and kind of hate them at the same time."

He took a sideways step closer to me, bumping our shoulders together. "I love you."

"You'd better, after this whole rescue mission." I bumped our shoulders together again. "Love you too."

~

The same sort of berries seemed to be in season as had been last time I was in this forest, though I was pretty sure it was a different time of year. I found them easily this time, without any help from crows; I think I was getting used to fairy land.

It would be a shame, almost, to leave.

I was thinking of going home as a forever thing. I'd walked right into fairy land, and I was preparing to walk right out, so it stood to reason I should be able to walk right back in again, whenever I pleased. But I didn't think fairy land ran on reason, exactly. I'd been all through the little woods in my hometown, or thought I had, a dozen times, and I'd never found myself in fairy land before Kai went missing.

It would be a shame to leave. But I wanted to be home. I wanted Grandma and Manda and my parents. My teachers and neighbors and the family in the pew behind us at church. Fairy land was cool. But home would be better.

We walked at whatever pace we pleased, eating handfuls of berries as we went. And it was nice. It felt like living in a game we'd played as children.

~

"I've completely lost track," Kai said. "What time of year is it? What time of year will it be when we get home?"

I shrugged. "I was going to ask the newspaper princess while we were there, but I forgot. I guess it must be midsummer, at least. Maybe nearly fall?"

"I hope it's still summer. It'll be hard, after all this, to go right back to school the next morning."

"It'll be hard going back to school no matter what. Maybe we'll graduate with the sophomores, if we're lucky. Probably we'll be in with the freshmen, by now." Well, with the class that were freshmen when we left. But Kai would know what I meant.

He stopped walking abruptly. "I changed my mind. Let's stay in fairy land."

"The freshmen aren't that bad."

"They were terrible. And how am I going to explain the gap on my college applications?"

"We could just get our GEDs, maybe. I don't know about the college thing—the same way we explain it to everyone else, I guess?"

We still hadn't decided. We hadn't really talked about it since the mountains.

"We'll figure it out," Kai said. "We have the photos, at least. Some of those look pretty magical, and they're just Polaroids, not some fancy thing that could have been altered."

"So you're thinking we tell the truth."

He frowned. "Well. Maybe we try? For Grandma and your parents at least, and if it works they can help us come up with a cover story for everyone else. You know I hate lying."

He did—to a fault. I did like the idea of being honest, too. I just wasn't sure it would be well received. "Okay, we'll try."

~

I had a feeling, that last morning. Something in the air, I guess. Something felt different.

As we walked through the woods that day it changed, blue moss fading into green, leaves falling into familiar shapes. We were home. We were nearly home. I felt a giddy sort of joy, but I didn't say anything—I kept forgetting, I suppose, how bad Kai's vision was without his glasses.

So it wasn't until we reached the edge of the trees, and stepped out at the base of a familiar hill, and the rushing river opposite it, that he realized where we were, recognizing the broad strokes of the landscape.

"We're here," he said.

"We're here," I agreed, and without any discussion we both took to running, until we were at the top of the hill, out of breath, but giddy and giggly and glad.

It was still midmorning, and I had lost track of the days of the week long ago, but I thought it might have been a school day; there was no one else about.

"Your house first," I asked, "or mine?"

He shrugged. "Does it matter? We share a front yard."

"True."

We made our way across town—I'm sure we looked quite a sight, Kai still wearing a mismatched pair of winter boots, and me still dressed like something out of a picture book. No one took notice of us, or perhaps we just took no notice of them—no one approached us, at least, and I hardly noticed if there was anyone about, all my focus on Kai beside me, and Mom and Dad and Grandma just a short walk away.

Our rosebush was blooming in the front yard, bigger than ever—it had been my job to trim it for years now, since it was difficult for Grandma as she aged, and my parents really were no good with gardening. It hadn't been trimmed, then, at all last year, or yet this year, and it always grew furiously. It had spread out so a few branches were dangling over each of our front porches, and it was so tall it nearly reached the second story windows.

There were several bees buzzing around it, and I was so happy, so happy.

Kai and I were still holding hands, as we had been almost always since I'd found him—a little because I just didn't want to let him go, but also because he couldn't see well enough to know where he was going without me. We let go of each other, now, and I went to ring my front doorbell, and he went to ring his.

I had a moment of panic, as the sound echoed—what if they were at work? They were probably at work. What if I had to come sit in Grandma's kitchen while she called their offices, and what if they didn't want to leave work early to see me?

Mom opened the door.

"Gerda?"

"Hi, Mom."

She threw herself around me. "Oh, Gertrude. Oh, sweetheart. We thought you were dead."

By the time Dad came to see what the commotion was about, we were both crying, and then he wrapped his arms around both of us, and he was crying, too.

"Gerda!" Kai called. "Come show Grandma you're all right."

And so I ended up in Grandma's kitchen after all, but with Mom and Dad there too, all of us sitting around the table crying, while Kai ran up to his room to find his spare glasses. And Grandma hugged me, and Mom hugged me, and Dad, and Kai, and we were home. There were stories to tell yet, and questions to ask, and unexplainable things to explain. But we were home. Kai laced his fingers through mine beneath the table, and smiled at me, eyes sharp and focused, finally, behind his glasses. And Dad wrapped an arm around my shoulders, and we were home. We were home.

Acknowledgements

Special thanks to my patrons, Jeff and Sue Prater, Sam Medlock, Lynn and Lowell Nystrom, Beth and Steve Cragle, and Jamie Krause. And extra special thanks to Sue Prater, who is not only my Patron and my mom, but also my copyeditor.

(Also thanks to Hans Christian Andersen for writing *The Snow Queen*.)